“Let’s

“What should we do?” Abby asked.

“Sunday service? We’ll appear to talk with each other...but not too much.” Nate ran his fingers through his brown locks. “If some other fellow shows too much interest in you, I’ll be sure to join the two of you and pretend to be jealous.” He was grinning when their gazes met.

His explanation caused her to feel a little flutter inside. She knew he was teasing her, but the thought of him wanting to ward off other suitors pleased her...even if it wasn’t real.

Nate stood up. “I guess we should head back.” He held out his hand and she accepted his help to rise. His fingers felt warm and wonderful against hers.

They exited the house the same way they came in. Nate opened the buggy door for Abby and helped her climb in.

Being this close to Nate made it difficult for her to think, to breathe evenly, but she did. The man had agreed to help her out. She couldn’t forget that it was nothing more. Her heart had already been broken once, and she wouldn’t let that happen again.

Rebecca Kertz was first introduced to the Amish when her husband took a job with an Amish construction crew. She enjoyed watching the Amish foreman's children at play and swapping recipes with his wife. Rebecca resides in Delaware with her husband and dog. She has a strong faith in God and feels blessed to have family nearby. Besides writing, she enjoys reading, doing crafts and visiting Lancaster County.

Books by Rebecca Kertz

Love Inspired

Loving Her Amish Neighbor
In Love with the Amish Nanny
The Widow's Hidden Past
His Forgotten Amish Love
A Convenient Christmas Wife
Their Fake Amish Betrothal

Women of Lancaster County

A Secret Amish Love
Her Amish Christmas Sweetheart
Her Forgiving Amish Heart
Her Amish Christmas Gift
His Suitable Amish Wife
Finding Her Amish Love

Visit the Author Profile page at LoveInspired.com for more titles.

THEIR FAKE
AMISH
BETROTHAL

REBECCA KERTZ

LOVE INSPIRED
INSPIRATIONAL ROMANCE

LOVE INSPIRED®
INSPIRATIONAL ROMANCE

Recycling programs
for this product may
not exist in your area.

ISBN-13: 978-1-335-93730-8

Their Fake Amish Betrothal

Copyright © 2025 by Rebecca Kertz

Love Inspired
22 Adelaide St. West, 41st Floor
Toronto, Ontario M5H 4E3, Canada
www.LoveInspired.com

Printed in Lithuania

MIX
Paper | Supporting
responsible forestry
FSC® C021394

Beloved, if God so loved us,
we ought also to love one another.
—*1 John* 4:11

For Katie Gowrie, a terrific editor,
for her insight and understanding.

Katie, it's a pleasure to work with you.

Chapter One

"Next stop, New Berne!" the bus driver announced over the loudspeaker.

Abigail Yost straightened in her seat, feeling suddenly nervous. She was on her way to begin a new life in Lancaster County, away from her family and the heartbreak of losing her betrothed to her sister. Clara's gloating over her current plans to marry in late August had been the last straw that had pushed her into action. Thankfully, Abby had been accepted for the position of schoolteacher in New Berne and the job came with a generous income and place to live.

The vehicle slowed to a stop, and Abby sprang to her feet and grabbed her valise. She exited the bus then stood in the parking lot of a busy shopping center and glanced around. Then she saw a middle-aged Amish man waving as he approached her from between parked cars.

"Abigail Yost?" the man asked. He wore a maroon shirt with black pants and suspenders. His beard was a mixture of brown and gray.

She relaxed when he gazed at her with warmth and kindness. "*Ja,* that's me." Abigail smiled at him. "Preacher Jonas Miller?" The church elder was the one who'd contacted her after she'd applied for the position. He looked to be the same age as her father.

"*Ja*, but Jonas will do." He reached for her bag. Not wanting to offend him, she allowed him to take it. "Did you have a *gut* trip?"

"It was fine," she said as she followed him to his buggy. "Took just over five hours to get here."

"You must be tired." Jonas placed her valise in the back of his buggy and then opened the door for her.

"Not at all. I napped for a bit after I ate the sandwich I made for the trip." She climbed onto the front passenger seat.

"Would you like to see the school?" he asked with a smile. "Or would you prefer I show you where you'll be living so you can relax and get settled in?"

"Can't I do both?" She couldn't wait to live in the teacher's house. She relished the thought of having a place of her own, free from the stress of living with her family. Her parents' support of Clara's relationship with Peter, despite knowing the man had claimed to love Abby and asked her to marry him six months before, had been deeply hurtful. They hadn't understood how difficult it was for her to watch Peter court her sister and plan their future.

But now, she had her own future to focus on. The first day of school was over two months away. Abby was grateful that Jonas had accepted her decision to come early and get situated in her new Amish community.

"I'll take you to see them, but both are still being worked on. They're not ready but they will be in plenty of time before *schule* starts." Jonas pulled out of the parking lot and turned onto the main road.

Abby became concerned. "If the cottage isn't ready, where will I stay?" She'd been so eager to leave New Wilmington that she hadn't thought of the consequences of arriving early. "Maybe I shouldn't have come this soon."

"*Nay*, we're glad you're here," he assured her. "It is a *gut* thing that you'll be able to get settled into your new community and meet new friends and neighbors before the work begins." He flashed her a grin. "My *dochter* Fannie owns a restaurant with an upstairs apartment. You can live there and have access to the kitchen downstairs and her delicious food. And best of all, you won't have to pay for any of it. It's the least we can do to make you welcome, especially since the *haus* that we promised isn't ready for you."

Widening her eyes, Abby gazed at his profile. "I'm grateful for her generosity."

"That's Fannie. She is warm and giving by nature," he assured her. "She can't wait to meet you. I think you'll enjoy being friends with her and the young women who work for her."

Unused to such kindness, Abby was unsure how to respond. Her family had always seemed distant to her, but here she was a stranger in a new town and she was treated as someone special, a valued teacher and member of this new community. Thoughtful, she became quiet as Jonas drove into the open countryside, past Amish farmhouses with acres of land. It was a lovely early summer day. The sun shone on lawns and crops, and there was a light breeze that teased the tendrils of her hair that had escaped from under her prayer *kapp*. Her spirits rose. This new beginning was exactly what she needed.

Compared to the lengthy bus ride she'd had, it didn't seem long at all before Jonas turned on the blinker and then pulled onto the driveway of a one-room schoolhouse. The outside of the building was made of white-painted brick, which had seen better days. Beyond it on the other side of the lane sat a cottage with the front door wide-open. The cottage looked newly built, with a small front porch perfect for sitting outside on days like this one when the weather was warm. They headed there first.

"As you can see, the *haus* is new. The outside is done but the interior isn't finished." He preceded her inside. "Nathaniel," he called. "You've got company!"

From somewhere in the back, she heard the man's reply. "I'll be right there."

Less than a minute later, a man entered the living room where she and Jonas stood. In his twenties, he wore black suspenders with navy triblend pants and a royal blue short-sleeved shirt that revealed muscled forearms. She could see his dark hair below his black-banded straw hat. He was startlingly handsome, with smooth cheeks that spoke of his unmarried status.

"*Hallo*, Jonas," he greeted warmly.

The preacher smiled. "*Hallo!* Is the work going well?"

"*Ja*, I'm insulating the exterior walls." His gaze strayed briefly toward her before he focused his gaze on Jonas.

"Abigail," Jonas said, "this is Nathaniel Hostetler. He's doing the work on the cottage and *schule*. Nate, this is Abigail Yost, our new *schule*-teacher."

"*Hallo*, Nathaniel." Abby smiled. "*Danki* for all you're doing here." She was excited; she couldn't believe she would be living in a brand-new house.

The warmth in Nathaniel's expression seemed to chill as he met her gaze before he quickly looked away. "*Gut* to meet you," he said.

Abby got the impression that he wasn't happy to see her, that her presence stirred him up somehow. "It seems as if you have a great deal of work ahead of you," she replied, all while wondering if she'd done something to upset him.

Was he embarrassed that she'd come before the house was finished?

He shrugged without making eye contact with her. "I'll get it done before school starts, don't you worry."

She wasn't sure how to handle the builder's cool welcome, so she didn't respond.

"We'll let you get back to it," Jonas said. "I'm going to show her the *schulehaus* before we head over to the apartment above Fannie's Luncheonette."

The man's brown eyes warmed for the preacher as he nodded. "Do you need me to stop by your farm before I head home?" he asked.

Jonas shook his head. "*Nay*, Joshua and I have it covered. *Danki* for asking. Although I do miss having you there."

Nathaniel chuckled. "That's a nice thing for you to say."

Considering how coolly Nathaniel had greeted her, the sound of his good humor with Preacher Miller took Abby by surprise. She forced a smile. "I'm sure I'll be seeing you again, Nathaniel. Have a *wunderbor* day," she said before she turned and left the cottage. It took another minute for Jonas to join her outside.

"He seems pleasant," she said awkwardly as she and Jonas started toward the schoolhouse across the driveway. The man had been amiable with Jonas but not her. Abby wanted to ask him what Nathaniel's problem with her was but since she was new here, she wasn't about to stir up trouble. Besides, it wasn't as if he'd been rude—he just hadn't been warm.

"He is and he's a *fine* carpenter. He used to run a construction business with his *bruder* Aaron here in New Berne. Aaron decided to work for a major company in Indiana. They wanted to hire Nate as well, but Nate wasn't interested. When he expressed an interest in dairy farming, I hired him and was glad I did. Nate's a natural in the business. He's been with me for over three years now. It's been *gut* to have him as an employee. I believe he's thinking about buying a farm." Jonas shot her a glance. "He's a *wunderbor* young man."

A *wunderbor* young man who didn't care for her. With a mental shrug, Abby decided that she wouldn't let Nathaniel's attitude bother her. After all, she'd had her share of men who'd treated her poorly. She'd fallen hard and fast for Peter and had been excited about their courtship until his head was turned by Clara, and she'd been left heartbroken.

Perhaps it was just as well that Nathaniel clearly had no interest in her. She wasn't about to let another man into her heart anytime soon anyway. So she wouldn't let this builder and his coldness get under her skin.

The school was an old one, she saw as she walked with Jonas toward the building. The bricks were crumbling in places but otherwise, the building seemed sound. "What does he have to do here?" Abby lightly touched the area where the bricks appeared undamaged.

"He'll replace or shore up the loose bricks. He'll also spruce up the interior. Nate knows what he is doing. I have tremendous faith in his work and high standards." Jonas opened the door and gestured for her to precede him.

The interior was dull and gloomy. It was in desperate need of repairs and a new paint job. Studying it, Abby envisioned what it would be like after the school renovations were done and she'd readied the classroom for her students. She'd put up charts of the alphabet and numbers with a couple of simple arithmetic problems. Two bookcases would be nice to hold the textbooks and other reading material. The desk looked timeworn but it was in good shape. Once school started, she'd be teaching kindergarten through eighth grade, all in the same room.

She loved children, teaching them and watching them grow and learn. She'd volunteered in an Amish school back in New Wilmington. She enjoyed helping in the classroom, had substituted on occasion, and had always wanted a teaching position of her own. But there had been no full-time openings at that time. Plus, her family wouldn't have liked it. She earned more for the household working the two part-time jobs she'd had. They hadn't been able to keep her from volunteering, though. They couldn't complain too much when others within the community had praised her to her parents for her help.

"What do you think?" Jonas asked.

Abby smiled. "I can see it in my mind's eye all finished, and I know I'll enjoy teaching here."

He grinned. "I'm glad. It's been a while since the building was used. Years, in fact. Our *kinner* have had to attend a *schulehaus* on the eastern side of New Berne. The town is larger than you'd think, and it's difficult for parents to navigate the busy downtown streets. We'll be happy to have them closer to home."

"How did they get there?" She frowned.

Jonas studied his surroundings. "Parents had to take them by buggy. Some families took turns, but it made things difficult, especially during the winter months when their *kinner* had to miss *schule* because of the distance over bad roads. This will be much better for everyone." He faced her with a grin. "Would you like to see your temporary housing?"

"Ja. Danki." Abby wondered how far the apartment was from the school. There was much to be done before school started. She'd need supplies and the bookcases she'd en-

visioned but she wasn't about to ask for them on her first day here.

She followed Jonas outside to his buggy and climbed in while wondering about her living quarters and how she would get to and from the schoolhouse. It would all work out, she decided with optimism. *Gott* had given her this amazing opportunity to teach and she would make the most of it as she began her new life in New Berne, away from Clara and her parents who'd always seemed to favor her younger sister.

Nathaniel stood on the front porch of the unfinished cottage and watched the new schoolteacher chatting with Jonas as they exited the school and headed toward the buggy. The preacher said something that made the woman grin. He scowled. She was an attractive blonde with bright green eyes, a small nose and perfectly shaped pink lips, but he refused to be taken in by her pretty face—refused to be taken in *because* it was such a pretty face. If she'd been plainer, it would have been easier for him to be kind, but as it was, she reminded him of Emily, a woman he'd once cared for. Being used by the woman in his past had changed him and made him distrustful.

Heading back into the house, he went to work installing insulation between the wall studs. The plumbing for the kitchen and bathroom had been roughed in by a local plumber he and his brother Aaron had used, and Nate was more than familiar with the man. A propane tank would be installed in the back of the cottage for the refrigerator, stove and washing machine.

He frowned as his mind drifted from the job. Nate didn't want to be here. He'd never cared for construction when he'd worked with Aaron, although he managed to do it well.

If anyone other than Preacher Jonas had asked him to do the job, he would have turned them down. But he owed Jonas a debt of gratitude, so he'd known he couldn't say no, even if it meant delaying other plans that he'd made. He'd finally saved enough money to put a down payment on farm property, but now he had no time to search for any until the cottage and school were done. He tried to look on the bright side and remind himself that he was being paid well and could add to his savings, but the wait to begin his new life bothered him. He would be glad when this job was over.

He planned to finish it as quickly as possible so he could focus on his real goal—a dairy farm of his own. Thanks to Emily's duplicity in allowing him to court her even though she had no desire to marry him, he'd decided that he didn't want or need a woman in his life. All he required was something of his own to focus on. Something he could invest himself into that would keep him motivated and happy. Thankfully, Emily had moved away, and he felt free to chase his dreams without having to see her again. It was Preacher Jonas who had given him a purpose when he'd hired Nate to work on his dairy farm. Nate had loved the job and decided on a plan for his future with Jonas's encouragement.

With the windows open to allow a breeze, Nate heard buggy wheels on the driveway close to the cottage a short time later. Curious, hoping that it wasn't Jonas and Abigail returning, he stepped onto the porch as a buggy parked close by. He recognized Fannie in the driver's seat. When she didn't get out, Nate went to see what she wanted.

"Nate, have my *dat* and the new schoolteacher been here yet?" she asked.

"*Ja*, they've come and gone some time ago." Nate saw her frown. "What's wrong?"

"I just found the apartment key in my purse! I brought it home by mistake. I'd bring it to the restaurant but I have a doctor's appointment, and I'll be late if I do." Her gaze pleaded with him. "Would you be able to take it to my *dat*?"

Nate thought of all the work he had left to do today, but he understood that with her in the family way, it was important for her to go for regular checkups. Besides, he wanted a break from the job anyway. "*Ja*, I'll take it."

Fannie looked relieved. *"Danki."* She handed him the key through the open window of the buggy. "I owe you one."

"*Nay*. Not when you've given me so much free food over the last four years." He grinned. "But I hope that doesn't stop you from sharing a sweet or two."

She laughed. "You're always welcome to anything I make, Nate. I'll get in touch later this week. I'd like to have you over to dinner. I know my husband, David, will enjoy spending time with you." Fannie eyed the cottage. "Between the *haus* and *schule*, you certainly have your work cut out for you. I know you're the best man for the job."

He nodded in appreciation of her comment. It was nice to hear his work was valued, even if construction wasn't something he really enjoyed. "I'll get this key over to Jonas."

"I appreciate it." With a wave, Fannie steered her buggy toward the road.

After Fannie left, Nate locked up the cottage and school before he drove over to her restaurant.

When he arrived at Fannie's Luncheonette, he hitched his horse to the post in the rear of the property. He climbed down, tied up his gelding and then went into the building through the back door.

"Hallo!" he called as he stepped into the back hallway.

"Nate!" Linda King came out of the kitchen and smiled at him. "This is a surprise."

"It's *gut* to see you, Linda," he said warmly. "Sorry to come in after closing. I have the key to the apartment for Jonas. Is he here? Fannie found it in her purse—she forgot she'd brought it with her."

"Praise the Lord," she said with a grin. "I tried to call Fannie after I looked but couldn't find it." She gestured toward the front room. "*Ja*, Jonas is here. He figured there was a mix-up. He is in the dining room with Abigail, enjoying pie and coffee, hoping that Fannie will return with it. Want to join them?"

"*Danki*, but I have work to do yet at the cottage before I head home." He started toward the room, then stopped abruptly and faced her. "Pie and coffee to go?"

"Of course," she said with a grin. "They'll be ready in a minute."

Nate entered the front dining room and spied Abigail and Jonas seated along a side wall. "Jonas," he greeted. He held up the key. "Fannie asked me to bring this to you."

The preacher smiled. "I'm glad you're here. I need to get back to the farm. I'm already later than I expected to be. Would you mind showing Abigail the upstairs apartment?"

Nate's gaze strayed briefly to the woman seated across from Jonas. Trying not to show how he felt about being put on the spot, he forced himself to smile politely. "I'll be happy to."

Jonas appeared relieved. "I appreciate this, Nate. I know Abigail wants to get settled in."

The preacher departed, leaving him alone with Abigail Yost. "Follow me," he said. The woman got up from the table and trailed him down the hall. He tried to not be resentful of her as he climbed the steps and opened the door on the top landing. It wasn't her fault that he had to finish the cottage and renovate the school. It was annoying that she had come six weeks earlier than expected, but that didn't change the task in front of him. He'd have been working on the two buildings regardless of whether she was here or not. And as for showing her the apartment, he couldn't blame the lost work time on Abigail since it was Jonas who'd asked him for the favor. Still…

Nate stepped back and allowed Abigail to see her new temporary home. "It's small but has everything you need except for a stove."

"I don't need you to show me around," she said stiffly.

"I don't mind," he insisted, as politeness required. He wouldn't want her reporting back to Jonas that he'd been rude.

He heard her sigh heavily. "Fine." She meandered about the small space. "Preacher Jonas said that I'd have restaurant kitchen privileges."

He nodded. "That's *gut*. Fannie is an excellent cook. You'll have plenty of opportunity to enjoy the food while living upstairs. Is there anything you need?" he asked.

Abigail averted her glance. "*Nay*, I'm fine. *Danki*."

"Your bag?"

"*Ach*, it's downstairs. I'll get it."

He sighed inwardly. "Where is it?"

"In the kitchen." She turned as if to head downstairs.

"Abigail." His voice came out sharper than he intended. "I'll get it. Why don't you look around and see what else you might need while you're living here. *Ja?*"

"*Fine,*" she snapped without meeting his gaze.

He couldn't help staring for a moment before he turned away and hurried downstairs to retrieve her bag.

Back upstairs, Nate stood in the entryway to the apartment. "Here you go." He looked around the living area. "Where would you like it?"

"In that corner," she said crisply, pointing to the corner closest to the door. "I appreciate you letting me inside and getting my suitcase, but I'm sure I've taken up too much of your time." Without another word, she seemed to dismiss him as she headed to the window and peered outside.

Nate studied her for a long moment. He knew he hadn't handled this well, but he couldn't think of how to fix it. Finally, the awkwardness in the silence became too much to bear. "I've left your key on the counter. Have a *gut* rest," he said before he shut the door behind him and hurried down the steps.

Linda met him in the hallway with a container and a to-go coffee cup. "Here you go, Nate."

He smiled at her as he took his order and handed her the money owed. "Thanks, Linda. Say hi to Esther for me."

"I will," she replied.

Nate left and headed back to the teacher's cottage. He planned to work another two hours before calling it a day. There was no need to rush home when nothing was waiting for him there. He lived alone in the house once owned by his grandparents who'd left it to him and his older brother. He and Aaron had worked and lived together until his brother decided to join a large construction firm in another state, leaving Nate the sole resident.

The rich scent of coffee filled the interior of his buggy. He was eager to drink it while he ate his pie. He wondered what kind of pie Linda had given him.

As he took the main road out of town, he couldn't stop thinking about the new schoolteacher. She truly looked quite a lot like Emily, and his mind drifted back to the horrible memory of when she'd rejected his marriage proposal, claiming she wasn't cut out to be a farmer's wife. Then she'd told him she'd accepted a job offer in a new community. Only a few months after leaving New Berne, she'd married someone else. Nate had been heartbroken. He'd felt as if Emily had been playing with his affection. Why had she allowed him to court her if she'd never envisioned a future with him?

He'd worked hard to put her out of his mind in the time since then, but seeing the new schoolteacher brought it all back. Why had Abigail come so early? Nothing was ready for her. Not the schoolhouse nor the cottage. What would make someone show up six weeks before a job began? Was she running from something? Or was she simply eager to start her new life in his Amish community?

Nate felt a sniggle of irritation. He hoped she didn't plan on making a daily check on the construction progress. He preferred to be alone while he worked. He didn't need her getting in his way and messing with his head, the way pretty women always did. He'd been taken by a woman with a beautiful face before and he wasn't about to get involved with one again. He planned to avoid her as much as humanly possible while he did his work as *quickly* as possible so he could get done and move on with his plans.

Chapter Two

Abby woke up and studied her surroundings. The opaque, forest green window shades did much to keep the room dark, except for slivers of sunlight peeking from each side. Curious about the time, she got out of bed and pulled up one edge of the window covering to peer outside. The position of the summer sun suggested that it was still early. She turned on the battery lantern on the bedside table and then dressed. Wanting to let in the sunshine, she tugged up the window shade and smiled as she looked at her surroundings in daylight.

A mirror hung on the wall, and she checked her reflection to ensure her blond hair was neatly rolled and pinned under her *kapp*, her head covering different than the heart-shaped ones the women wore here in New Berne. She studied her features critically. Her green eyes seemed too big for her face and her nose too short. She'd never been the pretty sister—that had been Clara. But it did no good to fret about that.

When she was ready for the day, she made her way downstairs to find two young women working in the kitchen. She recognized Linda from yesterday.

The other woman was blond and pregnant. Fannie, Abby thought.

"*Gut mariga*, Abigail," the expectant mother said. "I'm Fannie, Jonas's *dochter*."

"It's nice to meet you. Please call me Abby." She smiled. "*Danki* for allowing me to live here until the cottage is finished."

"It's my pleasure to have you here," Fannie said. "Are you hungry? I can make you an omelet. We also have breakfast casseroles or muffins. Whatever you'd like. I have a coffee cake in the oven, too."

Abby was grateful for the welcome and the young woman's warmth. "A muffin and coffee will be fine." Her eyes widened when Jonas's daughter handed her a plate with three muffins with a mug of the fragrant brew.

Fannie chuckled. "You can keep what you don't eat in your apartment."

"That's *recht*," Abby teased. "I live upstairs now."

"The luncheonette isn't open yet. Why don't you sit and relax in the dining room." Linda opened the oven door to check on the coffee cake. "Unless you'd rather take it to your room."

"I prefer to eat down here," Abby said as she gazed longingly at the muffins. Her mouth watered at their delicious smell. "What time does the place open?"

"Not for another hour yet," Fannie told her.

"Okey." Abby started to leave the kitchen, then halted and faced the two women. "The schoolhouse is some distance away. Is there a bus I can take to get there?"

Fannie stopped peeling potatoes and met Abby's gaze with raised eyebrows. "Didn't my *dat* show you the pony cart in the stable out back?"

"Nay. There's a vehicle I can use?" She was relieved. "Just until I'm able to purchase one myself, of course."

"No need to buy one," Fannie assured her. "No one uses

it anymore. It was sitting in my *dat*'s barn. The church elders had it fixed up for you." Fannie grinned. "And there is a horse to go with it. A mare. Jennie's not a young one but she still has a lot of life in her." She started to chop the potatoes she'd peeled. "Enjoy your breakfast and then I'll show you where it is."

"*Danki*, Fannie," Abby said, blinking back tears of gratitude. "You all have been so kind to me."

"We're happy you're here," Fannie said. "It's been too long since our young ones had a school here. The old school was destroyed in a storm when I was young girl. The building we have now was moved to our village three years ago, but it needed too much work for us to use it, and there was little money at the time to fix everything. We spent the time since then raising the money for the cottage and renovations. That we could find and hire you is a blessing for us. It was difficult getting our *kinner* to the only other Amish school on the far side of town."

"It's a blessing for me, too," Abby murmured.

She entered the dining room with her coffee and muffins and took a seat closest to the hallway. Closing her eyes, she offered up a prayer of thanks to *Gott*. If not for Him, she would never have seen the newspaper employment ad for an Amish schoolteacher in New Berne while she'd been at the store. The ad requested that any applicants send a letter of interest to them.

Abby hadn't waited until she got home. She'd purchased paper and pencil at the store, and then taken a seat at the soda counter to write the letter. When she was done, she'd mailed it right then and there. A letter in return had arranged for a phone call, which she'd made from a pay phone at that same store. She'd spoken to Preacher Jonas Miller of New Berne, who was kind as he asked questions about whether she was betrothed, her age, her willingness to move, and whether she enjoyed working with children as well as her experience in the classroom.

Her answers must have satisfied him, because the preacher explained the benefits of the job and hired her on the spot. They'd come up with a date for her arrival, and he'd promised to meet her at the bus stop. She'd felt as if she were floating on air when she'd hung up the phone.

Pulling her thoughts from the past, Abby ate a chocolate chip muffin, closing her eyes as she savored the delicious combination of cake and chocolate. Linda brought in a small carafe of coffee and set it on her table. Abby thanked her and continued to enjoy her breakfast until she'd eaten two muffins, saving one to take upstairs with her.

She got up from the table and headed toward the kitchen with her dishes. "These were *wunderbor*! I saved one for later. I can't believe I ate two of them." She laughed. "Now I feel full enough to burst!"

Fannie chuckled. "Which flavor did you like the best?"

"The chocolate-chocolate-chip. I ate the regular chocolate chip first and loved it, but then when I had the chips with the chocolate cake...yum!" She grinned and held up the plate with the last muffin. "Would you mind wrapping this up for me?"

"I'll be happy to." Fannie took the plate and placed the last muffin in a foil container with a plastic lid after adding one more.

"Oh, you didn't have to do that!" Abby exclaimed.

"We have plenty." Fannie handed the tin. "My *vadder* did tell you that you can have anything you'd like to eat at any time, *ja*? I don't have to be here. Help yourself whenever you're hungry."

Abby frowned. "*Ach*, but that doesn't feel right."

"Abigail," Fannie said with fake sternness.

"Abby," she invited.

Fannie nodded. "Abby, I mean it. I'll show you where everything is, and if it makes you feel better, I'll leave you some meals in the refrigerator with your name on them. But you have kitchen privileges, so please take advantage of anything. *Oll recht?*"

Abby smiled. "*Danki.* I'm going to take the muffins and finish my coffee upstairs, and then I'll be down so you can show me the pony cart." She went up to her apartment. There, she placed the foil container in the corner of a countertop that ran along one wall. Then she pulled a chair close to the window to look outside as she finished her coffee. When she was done, she carried her empty mug down the steps toward the kitchen just as the back door to the restaurant opened, and Nathaniel Hostetler walked in.

Abby felt her heart race. "Nathaniel," she said with surprise.

His eyes widened as he met her gaze before it seemed to narrow. "Abigail."

She managed a smile. "Did you come for breakfast?"

He nodded abruptly. "*Ja*, Fannie makes the best sausage casserole."

"I ate her muffins this morning," she said. "They were *wunderbor.*"

His expression seemed to soften. "She is a *gut* cook for sure and for certain."

Fannie came out of the kitchen. "Abby, are you ready?"

"*Ja,*" she said with a grin.

"Nate!" Fannie exclaimed. "I didn't see you there."

"I couldn't resist stopping for one of your breakfast casseroles," he said warmly.

"Sausage?"

He laughed. "You know me so well."

"Linda can get one for you. Linda!" Fannie called out. "Nate's here for his breakfast. He wants his regular."

Linda peeked around the corner and smiled when she saw him. "Coming up. You want coffee, too?"

"*Ja, danki*, Linda." He faced Abby again with a smile that didn't look genuine to her. "Have a nice day."

Abby tried not to let his behavior bother her. She made her face impassive as she responded, "You, too."

Why didn't he like her? And why should she let it bother her? She had the job she'd always wanted, and a fresh start away from her family. That was what mattered. Not this surly construction worker with the unexplained grudge. She'd be cordial with him when she saw him around town— after all, New Berne was her home now and she'd work hard to be accepted by the community. But she'd never let a man's rejection sting her the way Peter's had.

She followed Fannie out the restaurant's back door to what looked like a lean-to on the left side of the property. The pony cart and horse were inside the barn. "This mare is yours."

"I appreciate this, Fannie. I don't know what else to say, but if you ever need help at the restaurant at any time before *schule* starts, I'll be happy to pitch in."

Fannie gave her a soft smile. "I may take you up on that if one of my girls can't make it in. But don't feel like you have to do anything extra. I'm glad to have you here."

"And I'm glad to be here," Abby assured her. At long last, she felt as if she was exactly where she belonged—no matter what Nathaniel Hostetler thought about it.

Nate waited for Linda to fix his breakfast and silently scolded himself for being surprised to see Abigail as he came in. She lived here, and if he continued to stop for breakfast or lunch, he would have to expect that he would see her often. But somehow, he'd managed to block that idea from his mind. Perhaps because something about the new schoolteacher bothered him more than he wanted to admit. After Emily had hurt him he'd become distrustful of women, especially single, pretty women.

"I added some home fries with onions." Linda's eyes twinkled as she handed him his food. "I know how much you like them."

"Much appreciated." With his coffee cup and take-out food in hand, Nate left the building and headed toward his buggy. He heard laughter from the barn nearby and presumed Fannie and Abigail were inside. He wouldn't stop to chat as he had work to do back at the schoolhouse.

When he'd hopped into his buggy, Nate steered it out of the parking lot and around the building, heading toward the school and cottage. He wished he could stay outdoors, but there was construction to be done and the sooner he finished it the better. First thing, with the help of his friend Jed, he would install Sheetrock on the wall studs. Once that job was done, he'd start spackling the next day. And while each coat of the joint compound dried, he'd head to the school to figure out what supplies he'd need to fix that building up.

The coffee was the way he liked it, with a hint of cream and two spoons of sugar. He sat on the cottage floor as he sipped from the brew and ate his sausage casserole. The scent alone of his breakfast was enough to make his mouth water. No other place made breakfast casseroles like Fannie's. With the plastic fork Linda had provided him, he took his first bite and moaned with appreciation. It was worth stopping for breakfast occasionally, even if he had to see the new schoolteacher. *Ja*, he decided, it didn't matter whom he saw or didn't see at Fannie's Luncheonette. Fannie Troyer's food was that good.

Just as he was finishing his breakfast, Nate heard the rumble of a truck on the lane. With a smile, he went to meet the delivery guys with the Sheetrock and other building supplies he'd been expecting. He'd come to know the two delivery men because of all the other supplies they'd brought to the site since he started the new house.

"Mike. Travis," he called out as he watched them drive their boom truck as close as they could get to the front porch. "Good to see you. I hope you have everything I ordered."

"You know we do," Mike said with a grin from the truck's open window. When the truck was close enough for them to use the boom, Mike took the drywall cart from the truck. "Where do you want them?"

"In the first room through the front door and a few pieces toward the back," Nate told them. The front room was the biggest area in the cottage. It would serve as the teacher's living room.

Travis took out two buckets and set them on the porch out of the way. Then Mike got into the truck and lowered the boom filled with Sheetrock level with the front decking.

"Have you got my drywall screws and glue too?" Nate asked as the two men began to load the cart with sheets of drywall.

Mike faced him with a smirk. "Have we ever let you down?"

"Not yet, but who knows what will happen before this place is done." Nate grinned to show them he was teasing before he followed them into the house after grabbing one bucket of spackle. He placed it in the kitchen area and then directed the two men to where he wanted the drywall.

Nate exited the house after the two and signed their delivery slip, tipping them well. As the truck left, he watched as Abigail Yost drove a pony cart to the school and tied up her horse. His jaw went rigid with tension. Great. The last thing he needed was her dropping by and checking on his work. As if she didn't trust him to get everything done properly. *Be polite*, he told himself as he walked in her direction.

Would she be upset that he hadn't started on the school yet? He'd needed to reach a point in the cottage construction before he could shift over to work in the classroom, but she probably wouldn't understand that. It wasn't as if he didn't have enough weeks to renovate the schoolhouse. They'd both be finished in plenty of time for her to move into her new house before the first day of school. If he had his way, he'd be back inside a dairy barn. Nate missed the sounds of the cows mooing in the milking shed, the scents that most people thought too pungent for their tender noses but not him. He became more irritable as he approached her.

"What are you doing here?" he asked when he was close enough to confront her face-to-face. That had come out harsher than he'd intended, and he hid a wince. Jonas wouldn't be pleased with him if he knew that Nate had snapped at the new teacher.

She blinked at him. "Excuse me?"

"I asked what you're doing here." He worked at making his voice sound less harsh this time, but he couldn't quite keep himself from scowling. Nate knew he shouldn't feel this way, but every time he saw the new schoolteacher, he became irritated.

She looked so much like Emily. He experienced a painful pang in the center of his chest.

"I wanted another look at the school," she said with a

narrowed gaze. "I'm going to work here. And live here. Which means I have a right to be here." She crossed her arms.

"Are you going to stop here every day?" he asked, trying to control himself.

"Maybe." She glared at him. "If I feel the need."

He gritted his teeth. "What need?"

"It's none of your business, but if you must know, I need to make plans for the first day of school." She gave him a challenging look. "So, you'd better get used to seeing me here often."

"Great," he mumbled as he turned around.

"What is your problem with me anyway?" she said, her voice tight. "I haven't done anything to you."

He stopped and faced her. "There's no problem. I have no thoughts whatsoever about you, *schule*-teacher." Then he stomped off, back to the cottage.

Nate knew he should apologize to her, but he couldn't make himself do it. He'd have to say he was sorry eventually, but he didn't have to right now.

Chapter Three

"Rude man," Abby grumbled after Nathaniel walked out of the school. Feeling agitated, she paced the one-room schoolhouse. "Who does he think he is? I have the right to be here. I'm the new teacher. What is his problem?"

She breathed deeply to calm herself. She'd come here for a reason, to see what she could do with the space. Eyeing the dingy walls, she decided that before they were painted, they needed a good scrubbing. Tomorrow she'd bring a bucket and soap after checking whether the hand pump out back worked. If not, she'd have to bring water with her. Abby figured she'd bring a tape measure or yardstick to measure the size of the bookcases she'd need before she made her request to Jonas.

"Wait until he finds out he needs to build me new shelves." Her smile was grim. She wasn't ready to tell him yet. She'd suffered enough of his poor attitude. Maybe she could discuss it with Jonas first and let him be the one to tell Nathaniel.

Abby went to the desk and opened the drawers to look inside. They were empty but not for long. She grinned as she thought about the supplies she'd store there. Pencils, chalk, paper and stickers were just a few items she planned to buy. By the time she'd finished her assessment of the space, it was getting close to lunchtime. She was hungry, so she left the building, unhitched her horse and climbed into her pony cart, refusing to look at the cottage where the man worked as she drove toward the road. He was the last person she wanted to see right now. While she'd love to see the progress in the cottage, she decided she'd wait until another time, preferably when Nathaniel Hostettler was absent.

"I'll ask Jonas for keys to both buildings." She grinned. Wouldn't Nathaniel be happy about that? *Nay*, he wouldn't be, but she didn't care. Her life was invested in these two buildings and the students she would have come September.

Abby decided to stop at the local general store, Kings, to pick up a few things she needed. Pulling into the lot, she drove to the hitching post and mentally made a list of items to buy as she tied up the mare and then headed inside.

"Gut mariga!" a woman said from behind the cash register.

She returned her smile. *"Gut mariga!* Lovely day, *ja*?"

"It is." The woman slipped out from behind the counter. "May I help you find something?"

"I need a few things for the apartment where I'm staying. Some soap for the shower. A couple of towels. Those kind of things."

The storekeeper perked up at her list. "New apartment. You don't happen to be living upstairs at Fannie's?"

Abby blinked. "I am. Why?"

"So, you're the new *schule*-teacher?" After Abby nodded, the woman's face lit up. "I'm Rachel King. My husband, Jed, and I own and run this store. Linda King, who works for Fannie, is my niece. And I have mail that came for you from New Wilmington two days ago."

Abby was stunned. She had told her parents where she

was going as she headed out the door, but she'd never expected to hear from them so soon. It was as if they had known beforehand where she was going and when. Had they found and read her correspondence with Jonas? Abby glanced at Rachel. "But I got here only yesterday."

The woman grinned. "Perhaps your *mam* and *dat* miss you and needed to tell you that," she said as she went back behind the counter and dug for something below it. "Or to wish you the best at your new position."

Abby silently thought *nay*, her parents wouldn't miss her. They hadn't seemed bothered at all by the fact that she was leaving home for a job far away, even though it meant they might not see each other again for a long time. She had no desire to return for a visit, and she knew they would never spend a dime to visit their "other" daughter. Abby's sister, Clara, had become the cherished daughter from the moment she entered the world. Even at only four years old, Abby had noticed the care and love shown to Clara was different from how their mother treated Abby. She always had to work harder and longer to gain her *mam*'s attention and love. Was it because Clara was more beautiful? More sweet and good-natured? Still, was that a good enough reason for a mother to so openly favor one daughter over another? Her father had treated her better than her mother, but more times than not he sided with his wife about every aspect of Abby's life.

"Aha!" Rachel exclaimed as she popped up with an envelope in hand. "Here it is." She handed her the letter.

"Danki." Abby studied the New Wilmington return address with the name "Yost" as the sender. She stuck it into the waistband of her apron. "I'll read it later," she explained. "I should get what I need and head home." She managed a chuckle. "My temporary home, that is."

With Rachel's help, Abby was able to find everything she needed to be comfortable. She saw that the store carried handmade prayer *kapps* like the ones the women wore here. Later, she would come back to buy one. She paid the storekeeper for today's items with the money she'd managed to save from the jobs she'd had over the last few years and then left for the apartment.

Most of her paychecks when she'd worked at the bakery and then the general store back in New Wilmington had gone to her parents. She'd accepted their claim that the money was needed to help with expenses for her care, but it had always bothered her that her younger sister had never been forced to work or pay a dime to them. Apparently, it didn't matter how much Clara's care cost. Only Abby was treated as a burden, with the need to pay for her keep. And so she had worked—and turned most of her wages over dutifully. Still, she was allowed to keep a small share—and there were a few occasions when she'd received a tip from a customer at the bakery and kept it hidden away. Once Abby had made the vast mistake of wishing aloud that she be allowed to keep more of her hard-earned money. But one sharp rebuke from her *mam* had taught her to keep her mouth shut or be treated to days of silent treatment from her parents and her only sibling. Why couldn't she have been more like Clara? Maybe then they would have loved her more.

As she drove home Abby thought of the letter waiting to be read. She was almost afraid to see what it said. But her heart dared to hope... Could her family miss her? Maybe they wished her well, or even planned to come for a visit. She waited until she was upstairs with the door closed and she had a chocolate chip muffin in her hand. She pulled out the envelope and took a hefty bite of sweetness before she opened it up and slipped out its contents. Abby realized what it was as soon as she saw it, and she felt sick to her stomach as tears filled her eyes.

It was not a letter from her parents. It was a wedding invitation...from Clara and Peter.

She tossed it on the floor and got up to pace the room. Why would her sister send it now? The wedding wasn't for months yet. Was this Clara's way of proving to her that she was the one Peter loved? As if Abby didn't know that already. Despite having everything she ever wanted, Clara had still gone after the one thing that had made Abby happy...her relationship with Peter.

Her family and their community had known that Peter had asked Abby to marry him and she'd accepted. Their relationship had been no secret. Peter had never said that he'd loved her...and yet she'd believed that he cared for her in his own way, and she'd thought they could be happy together. Peter, a widower, had lost his first wife with their unborn baby after she'd become sick and died of cancer in the early months of her pregnancy. Peter had wanted Abby as his wife and the mother of his future children, and she had looked forward to the idea of building a family with him. After all, Abby had been in love with Peter.

That love had ended the day she'd discovered Peter and Clara had been meeting secretly. Feeling betrayed, Abby had confronted Peter, who'd calmly told her that he and Clara were desperately in love. A love he had never felt for Abby. He'd chosen her because he'd thought she was a hard worker who would be a good mother, but when he'd fallen in love with Clara, he'd realized he wanted her as his wife and the mother of his children, not Abby.

And how on earth did her sister find out so quickly where she'd be living?

Abby had a craving for a cup of tea and welcomed the excuse to leave the apartment to get some hot water. The air had felt stifling since opening Clara's envelope.

She went downstairs and entered the kitchen. "May I have a cup of hot water?" she asked. "I bought tea bags. I thought about buying a teakettle since the apartment has electricity but I didn't want to overstep."

"Of course, you can have hot water," Fannie said with a smile. "And feel free if you want to use a teakettle upstairs."

Abby watched as Fannie poured her hot water and handed her the mug. *"Danki."*

"Something's wrong," the young woman said.

She shook her head. "I'm fine. I received mail from home today."

Fannie stirred a pot of soup on the stove. *"Ach*, I see. You're missing your family. It's understandable."

Abby didn't correct her. Instead, she managed a smile. "I'm happy to make New Berne my home," she said, meaning it.

Fannie nodded, appearing pleased. *"Gut.* We want you here." She added some carrots to the soup. "Did you mean it when you said you'd work here when we need you?"

"Ja, of course. But you'll want to put me to work washing dishes or waiting tables rather than cooking, since I was never taught how to cook. I figured out how to make eggs and sausage when I lived at home. When I worked at a bakery, I learned to bake cupcakes and muffins. My *mudder* never taught me how to fix anything. But that's just as well." Abby chuckled. "She's terrible in the kitchen."

Fannie laughed. "I'd be happy to teach you."

"I can learn and work at the restaurant at the same time, if you'd like," Abby said.

"You honestly want to help out?" Fannie eyed her with warmth.

"*Ja, schule* doesn't start for months yet. There are things I need to do there before then, but I have plenty of time to help here."

"How soon do you want to fill in if I'm low on staff?" Fannie asked, considering her.

"Is tomorrow morning too soon?" Abby found she was eager to pitch in. She'd be living on her own in the teacher's cottage. Learning to cook well would be a big plus after she moved in.

"I'll have plenty of help tomorrow but might be short-handed next week. I'll let know you when I need you." Fannie stuck out her hand. "Deal?"

"*Ja*." Abby shook it. "*Danki*." She now had something else to look forward to. She would ignore her sister's wedding invitation and enjoy her life now. Time away from the schoolhouse and cottage meant avoiding Nathaniel.

She scowled. The man was rude and stubborn—another complication in life that she didn't need.

Seeing Abigail on school property earlier had bugged him. He'd heard a rumor about her when he'd gone to Kings Store to ask for Jed's help. It seemed she'd left her home community in a hurry after ending a relationship. Nate's jaw tightened, and he tried to push her from his thoughts. He had work to do. He couldn't worry about Abigail Yost. Fortunately, she hadn't stayed at the school long today, and if she returned, he resolved that he'd ignore her.

Nate was contemplating where to start when he heard footsteps on the front porch. Likely Jed King, who was going to help hang the Sheetrock with him today.

"Jed?" he called out.

"*Nay*, it's Jonas, but Jed is here. He's hitching up his horse at the post near the school." The preacher entered the cottage and whistled. "You've got a lot done here, Nate. Looks great."

"*Ja*, it's coming along." Nate smiled. "Jed and I will hang the Sheetrock and then tomorrow I'll start spackling. While the coats dry here in the cottage, I'll work on the *schule*."

"*Wunderbor!*" Jonas walked farther into the building. "There is something I need to discuss with you regarding the classroom. I'd like to see two bookcases in each corner behind the teacher's desk for textbooks and school supplies. I'm hoping you could build them for us."

"From floor to ceiling?" he asked with a frown.

"*Nay*, since there will be two of them," Jonas said, "but they need to be tall enough for five shelves each."

Nate nodded. "I can do that."

"*Gut, gut!*" Jonas started toward the front porch. "I recently assured Abby that you're a man who knows how to deliver." He smiled. "I'll leave you to your work."

So the schoolteacher had asked for the bookshelves. That rankled—not only was she checking up on him, now she was adding to his workload.

"Nate!" Jed entered as Jonas was leaving. "*Ach, hallo*, Jonas."

Jonas inclined his head. "Glad to see you, Jed. We appreciate your help today."

"I don't mind. It's been a while since I left construction to work in the store, and I found myself looking forward to doing something like this again." Jed glanced about the room. "Wow, this place looks great."

Nate eyed the open space that would be the cottage's living room. Directly behind it, there would be a cozy kitchen, and down the hall the plans included a bathroom with the bedroom next to it.

"It's *wunderbor*," Jonas said with a smile. "Well, I have things to do. Just thought I'd check in with Nate and see if he could add on a little project for me." The preacher left then, leaving Nate alone with Jed.

"An add-on?" Jed asked, looking curious.

"Bookcases in the school for textbooks and things," Nate told them. He hadn't even started on the schoolhouse yet and he was adding more to his to-do list.

"I stopped for a look at the *schulehaus* before I came in," Jed said. "If you need help with the renovations there, let me know."

"Appreciate it." Nate gestured toward the back of the cottage. "I thought we might begin with the kitchen. What do you think?"

"Start from the back and work our way up front? I can agree with that." Jed met his gaze.

Nate would be glad when this part of the construction was done. "Are you ready to get started?"

"Let's do it." Jed grinned. "I'll get my stilts."

They worked all day until they got all the Sheetrock glued and screwed. Jed left because his wife Rachel called and needed him at the store. Nate walked through the cottage rooms, pleased by the progress. There was still an hour left of daylight. He completed a coat of spackle on the kitchen and bedroom walls before he called it a day. Tomorrow he'd put a second coat on those two rooms before he worked on the first coat in the bathroom and living room.

He was hungry and tired by the time he was done and had cleaned up. Nate thought of stopping at Fannie's, but the restaurant was probably closed, and even if it wasn't, he wasn't in the mood to reencounter the new schoolteacher today. He decided to stop at Kings General Store and ask Jed for a ham-and-cheese sandwich on rye. He'd buy a cola and a couple of cookies to go along with it. Maybe a bag of potato chips.

Nate had to ride past Fannie's on his way to Kings. There was a light in the kitchen that gave him hope that Fannie was still there. He knew she often worked late to prep food for the next day's menu. If he was lucky, Abigail would be upstairs in her apartment. He decided to stop—the lure of Fannie's food too great to pass up, even if it risked interacting with the schoolteacher again. He tried to enter through the back door of the building as he usually did, but he couldn't get in. Taking a chance, he tapped lightly on the steel door and was rewarded when he heard the click of a lock before the door opened.

"Nathaniel!" Abigail gasped with surprise.

"Sorry," he said. "I saw the light and thought Fannie was still here."

She shook her head. "I'm afraid not. I was making something for supper."

He sighed. "I'll let you go, then."

"Are you looking for something to take home to eat?" she asked.

"I was, but I don't want to put you out." He was surprised when she waved him inside.

"I can get you what you need." She spun and entered the kitchen. The fact that she wasn't angry with him surprised him after their last encounter.

He studied her. She was being kind and not annoying. Why? But as he watched her, he realized that for some reason she seemed sad.

Nate followed her into the room and watched as she worked to make sandwiches.

"Do you like chicken salad on rye? Fannie made it and it's one of the best things I've ever eaten." She kept her eyes fixed on what she was doing.

"I do like it, and I agree that Fannie's is the best." He wondered what had changed her and made her so quiet.

"Do you want lettuce and tomato on your sandwich?" she called out politely from behind the open refrigerator door.

"Lettuce," he said. "No tomato. *Danki.*"

She flashed him a grin as she returned with pieces of lettuce that had been washed and torn into sandwich-sized pieces. "I don't like tomatoes on it either."

Nate was bemused by his experience in Fannie's kitchen with Abigail as his sandwich maker.

"Do you want to take a drink with you?" she asked. "What about potato chips?"

"Is there cola? I'll have a can of that. And I enjoy potato chips with sandwiches." He observed the way she wrapped his sandwich in white paper and placed it with chips in a bag. "I'm going to add some cookies for dessert. I hope you like chocolate chip."

"I do," he said. "*Danki* so much for this."

She gathered everything he was to take home and gave it to him. "Enjoy your supper." Then she grabbed her own plate of supper and brought it to the stairs that led to her apartment.

Nate watched her go. "Abigail?"

She paused on the steps to gaze down at him. For the first time, he noticed that she appeared exhausted and perhaps even a little gloomy.

Sensing her unhappiness, he found something like regret kick hard inside his chest. "I appreciate this," he said softly as he studied her. *"Danki."*

The woman gave an abrupt nod and continued upstairs,

leaving him to go and turn the inside lock before closing the restaurant's back door behind him.

He tried not to think about the schoolteacher as he drove home, focusing instead on what he and Jed had accomplished that day. Nate decided that if he was tired in the morning, he would sleep later than usual before heading back to work. Maybe that way, he'd miss Abigail Yost if she stopped by early. An all-around good idea, he thought. He was still shocked by how nicely she'd treated him—and by how sad she'd seemed. Almost teary-eyed. Something must have happened to upset her. Was it him? He didn't think so. Nate sighed. No doubt, Abigail Yost would be fine and would return to her annoying, intrusive self by tomorrow.

Unless he was wrong about her.

He recalled her initial anger, but the sadness in her pretty, green eyes most affected him. Now he really couldn't get her out of his mind.

Chapter Four

In the dark, quiet kitchen of Fannie's Luncheonette the next morning, Abby flipped on the light and put on water for tea. Fannie and her employees weren't due to arrive for another two hours, and she didn't want to put on coffee or make a mess. As the teakettle heated, she checked inside the refrigerator and smiled. She felt better today after a difficult night worrying about her sister's wedding invitation. She was tired from her interrupted sleep, but she was also very hungry.

Fannie had left a portion of breakfast casserole with her name on it. The instructions on it said to put it in the microwave for one minute. She'd never used a microwave or any electric appliances before but she knew they were allowed in businesses such as Fannie's. She followed directions to heat her food, then took her tea and meal upstairs to enjoy for an hour until the sun rose in the eastern sky. By the time she was done eating and had made her bed, Abby heard someone come through the back door downstairs.

"Fannie?" she called down.

"*Ja*, it's me," came the woman's reply.

Abby hurried down the steps to see Fannie already getting ready for her breakfast customers. "The casserole was delicious. *Danki*."

Fannie looked up from adding coffee to the basket on a drip pot and grinned. "Glad you liked it."

"When the coffee is done, I'd like to buy two cups." Abby entered the kitchen to watch Fannie work. Eventually she would be helping here, and she wanted to learn how things were done before being asked to work.

"You don't have to pay me, Abby." Fannie shook her head.

"I already had tea and the breakfast you fixed. I want to bring coffee to the *schule* for me and Nathaniel."

"*Ach*, in that case, the coffee for the *two* of you is free. Nathaniel is sacrificing a lot to finish the cottage and renovate the school."

"He is?" Abby hadn't known. She wondered what Nathaniel had sacrificed, but it seemed wrong to ask Fannie about it. The information seemed personal enough that she felt it should come directly from the man himself. And she doubted he'd trust her enough to tell her. Yet.

"*Ja*, he is." Her short reply confirmed that it was best not to ask. Fannie pulled the pot from under the drip, then filled two to-go cups. "Here." She handed them to her with lids along with small containers of half-and-half and a few packets of sugar.

Abby accepted them gratefully. "I appreciate this."

Fannie grinned. "Any time."

Soon Abby was in her pony cart heading to the school. The coffee cups were on the floor, wedged against the base of the bench with her bucket of cleaning supplies so that they wouldn't spill. Beside her on the seat was the yardstick she'd bought to measure for potential bookcases.

It was a glorious morning, with bright sunshine spreading over the green countryside and glinting off the windows of the *English* houses she drove by. The temperature was lovely. Abby had always enjoyed this time of year, and June was even nicer in New Berne than it was in New Wilmington.

It seemed like a quick trip to the school property, and she pulled onto the lane and tied her horse to the post behind the school. She saw Nathaniel's buggy near the cottage. She reached down to the floor to pick up the coffee cups with fixings and headed toward the house. The door was open.

Abby entered the cottage cautiously. "*Hallo.* Nathaniel?"

She realized the building was empty when she heard no sound, including the man's response.

"Maybe he's at the *schule*," she murmured as she left the house and headed there.

When she'd arrived, she hadn't noticed the school's door propped open with a toolbox.

"Nathaniel?" she called as she stepped inside.

"Ja?" Nathaniel's head popped up from behind the desk. "*Ach*, it's you," he said not unkindly as he stood. *"Gut mariga."*

"Hard at work, I see." She approached with a smile. "I brought you coffee."

He eyed her with surprise and then grinned. "Just what I need."

His expression made her catch her breath as it forced her to accept that Nathaniel Hostetler was a handsome man. Last night when he'd finally smiled at her was the first time she'd noticed. It'd been hard to note his good looks when he'd scowled at her all the time. He accepted the cup and added what he liked in it.

"I'll be right back." Abby left the school to get her yardstick. Nathaniel was leaving the building as she returned.

"What are you doing?" he asked, his eyes narrowing on the item in her hand.

She met his glance as she lowered the yardstick. "I need bookcases. I thought I'd measure for them."

He held her gaze, his expression unreadable. "There's no need. I've got it handled."

Abby blinked. "What do you mean?"

"Jonas asked me to build two bookcases, one in each corner behind the desk," he said bluntly. "I said I would. I already figured it out and don't need your help."

She frowned, ignoring his crisp tone. "He never mentioned it to me." She moved to put the yardstick on the desktop.

"Maybe he wanted to surprise you." His brown eyes softened.

Her heart warmed at the return of his good humor. "Maybe," she said. "I'll let you handle it, then." Abby eyed the room. "Do you know if the hand pump out back works?"

"*Ja*, it does." He stepped closer, and she detected a hint of soap combined with a scent that must belong only to him. "Why?"

"I brought cleaning supplies. I thought I'd wash the walls." Abby pulled her gaze from his to study her surroundings. "They are going to be painted, *ja*?"

"You don't have to do that." His tone drew her attention again.

"I want to do it, Nathaniel," she insisted softly.

"Nate," he said.

She nodded. "Nate." She bit her lip. "And I'm Abby." She moved to touch the closest wall. "It's dirty. Paint sticks much better to a clean surface." When he was silent, she looked at him. "I'll stay out of your way."

"I wasn't worried about that." To his surprise, he meant it. Since their interaction in Fannie's kitchen when she made him a sandwich, he no longer felt nearly as irritated by her. He was curious about her. He was beginning to think he might have unfairly lumped her in with Emily just because of their similar appearances. And the sorrow he'd sensed in her before he'd left had concerned him.

He watched her rub her hand over the wall, saw her scrunch up her nose adorably.

"I'll start this morning," she told him as she began to walk the perimeter of the room.

"Or I could wash them," he suggested. Nate saw her freeze before she met his gaze.

"You have enough to do...especially with the added work on the bookcases. Eventually, I'll be helping Fannie out in the restaurant, but she said that she doesn't need any help this week. Let me do what needs to be done while I can."

He nodded. "I have to put a fresh coat of spackle on the kitchen walls, so I'll leave you to it."

"Okey." She followed him outside and pulled out a bucket from her pony cart. He watched her a moment before he went to the cottage to work.

When he was done in the kitchen, he troweled a layer of spackle in the other rooms. By then, it was getting close to lunchtime. Wondering if Abby was hungry, he returned to the school. Abby had finished scrubbing the wall behind the desk and was now attacking the one that ran the length of the school on the right side. She had replaced her prayer *kapp* with a kerchief on her head, tied at her nape. He silently watched her for a moment as she worked hard, putting in a lot of elbow grease. She was so focused on the task that she hadn't registered his presence.

She dropped her scrub brush into the bucket and wiped her forehead with the back of her hand.

"Abby," he said gently.

She gasped and spun. "I didn't realize you were standing there."

"Sorry." He gave her a gentle smile. "You've been busy."

"Ja." She twisted her neck a bit as if to relieve pain. "Got the front done and this wall is almost completed."

"I finished my spackling in the cottage until the coat dries." He came further into the school. "It's lunchtime. Have you brought something?"

She blinked as if surprised by the passage of time. *"Nay.* I didn't think of it."

"I'm going to head to Kings General Store for a couple of things I need for the cottage. I can pick us up some sandwiches and whatever you want to drink." He studied the walls she'd cleaned, impressed with her work. She'd washed the baseboard, too.

She furrowed her brow. "You don't have to do that."

"I need to go there anyway. And if you're even half as hungry as I am, I'm sure you could eat." He moved up to the first wall she'd finished and ran his fingers across the surface. It felt smooth and looked a lot better than it had when he'd first examined the place.

Abby turned toward the door. "I'll get my purse—"

He touched her arm. *"Nay,* this is my treat." Nate smiled. "You fed me last night."

"I…ah…*danki.*" She seemed flustered, and he studied her with interest.

"Chicken salad again?" he suggested. "Unless you want a hamburger. They make the best burgers and I'll get us potato salad if you like it." He waited patiently for her response, noting her inner struggle in her expression.

She bobbed her head. "A burger sounds *gut.* I don't remember the last time I had one." She smiled. "And I do like potato salad."

After asking what she liked for condiments and hearing her preference for a drink, Nate left for Kings General Store.

Nate saw his friend Jed King as soon as he entered. "*Hallo*, there!"

"How's the cottage going?" Jed asked.

"Fine," he said. "I'm almost done spackling. I still need to sand everything, but before I know it, the rooms will be ready for painting."

Jed nodded. "What can I get for you?"

"I'm going to head in the back and order some food from Rachel." Nate glanced down the aisle that presented hardware including nails, doorknobs and a few items of supplies for the do-it-yourselfer. "Hey, do you have extra fine sandpaper?"

"We do. It's toward the back of the aisle. I can get it for you."

Nate smiled. "No need." He perused the aisle to see what else he might need until he got to the sandpaper. He decided to buy three packs for now to make sure he had enough for the cottage and to start in the school. He took a quick look at available doorknobs for later then picked up a box of trim nails and a pack of wood screws, which he brought back to Jed along with the sandpaper. "I'll be back to pay for these after I order lunch," he told him.

Rachel King was at the deli and food counter when he approached. "Nate! *Gut* to see you."

"Same here."

"How's the *schule* coming along?" She pulled a pad and pencil toward her.

Nate moved closer to the counter. "Haven't done much work on it yet. Been mostly concerned with finishing the

cottage. Abby came today to scrub the walls there, how-
ever. I think clean walls will be easier to paint."

"For sure and for certain," she said with a smile. "So,
what can I get you?"

"Two hamburgers and two sides of potato salad, please."
He looked at the packaged snacks on the shelf. He grabbed
two packs of chocolate cupcakes and placed them on the
counter.

"You're either awful hungry or you're buying for a
friend," Rachel said with a smile after she'd written down
his order.

"Buying for a friend," he said. "And we'll have two root
beers, too, if you have them."

She grinned. "Of course, we have them." She put hamburgers on the grill to cook and pulled out two cans of
soda. "Let me guess. These are for you and the new *schule-
teacher*."

Nate nodded. "*Ja*. We've been working hard." He frowned.
"How did you guess?"

"You said she was there today, scrubbing walls—and
you didn't mention anyone else being around. I like the
new teacher. She came into the store the other day, and she
seems nice." Her smile gave way to a concerned expression. "I had mail for her when she came in. She seemed
shocked to get any…and she didn't look pleased. It was as
if she hadn't expected to hear from anyone. Especially since
her letter arrived before she got here. The return address
was from her hometown of New Wilmington, so I assume
it was from family. I suggested that her parents missed her
and wanted her to know it, but from the look on her face,
I don't believe she thought that was true."

"Hmm. I hope her mail wasn't upsetting news." Nate
suddenly felt uneasy as he recalled Abigail's expression

the night before. Had it been sadness…or worry, perhaps for a family member who had taken ill?

He paid Rachel for the food and then went to the front to pay Jed for the sandpaper and box of nails along with the pack of screws he'd decided to buy also. As he waited for Jed to ring up his items, two women entered the store.

"I heard the new teacher is from out of town. I wonder why she came all this way to teach?" said the first woman, Maryann Yoder, a known busybody in town.

"Maybe she simply wanted a fresh start," Emma, Micah Bontrager's sister, suggested kindly.

He couldn't hear what else the two women said as they headed toward the back of the store together, but their conversation reminded him of his own questions. Why *had* Abby come all this way to teach?

As he drove back to the school, Nate didn't like the direction of his thoughts. He didn't know the new schoolteacher's story, so he had no right to judge her one way or another.

Still, he couldn't help but feel a sniggle of doubt creep in about Abby Yost. He'd like to know why she'd come to New Berne. Why she'd left her home and her family to work in a new place.

If I want answers, I'll have to ask her. It wasn't like he had anything to lose if he did.

Chapter Five

"**Y**ou're back." Abby smiled at him as Nate walked into the school, carrying a white bag and two cans of soda. "What do you have there?"

He was quiet as he put the bag on the desk and began to sift through its contents. She frowned as she watched him. He'd left in a good mood but now it seemed as if something had upset him.

"*Danki* for getting lunch," she said.

Nate met her gaze. "You're *willkomm*." He glanced around. "Not sure where we'll sit."

"How about we eat outside?" Abby suggested. "It's a beautiful day, and I believe there is an old picnic table out back."

"*Okey.*"

There was a picnic table on the far side of the rear of the school near an old swing set and playground. It wasn't in the best of shape, but it provided seats and a table so that was all they needed. Nate waited for Abby to sit first and then took a seat across from her. "I wasn't sure what kind of cake you liked," he said apologetically as he unpacked the food from the paper sack.

"I love chocolate." She pulled the tab on the soda can and took a sip. "And root beer."

Nate didn't say anything as he wrapped his hamburger.

Abby stiffened as she watched him. Why wouldn't he talk? They had chatted earlier and everything seemed okay. "What's wrong?" she asked.

He met her gaze, and there was something in his brown eyes that worried her. Nate seemed almost angry. Of course, they were strangers, so she might have been misreading his expression. But he certainly hadn't been scowling like that earlier. How could he change so fast after a trip to town to pick up supplies?

"Nate?"

The man shook his head. "I saw Rachel while I was in there. She said you received mail before you arrived. Are you running from something...or someone? Why would you come from so far away for a teaching position?"

She gazed at him in shock and then she grew annoyed. "What business is it of yours why I came here to work? I don't owe you an explanation." She grabbed her food, then slid out from the bench. "Have a *gut* day, Nathaniel Hostetler," she snapped. "Don't let my presence offend you and I won't let yours bother me."

Carrying her lunch as she strode through the grass, Abby wondered whether to head back to her apartment. The fact that Nate didn't apologize or come after her shouldn't upset her but it did. She'd received enough judgment at home, and she refused to put up with it now. She'd done nothing wrong except fall in love with man who'd deceived her. And it was still too painful to talk about it with anyone.

Seeing her pony cart tied at the post, she marched over, set the food on the floor and then turned her vehicle around toward her apartment. She'd find her peace while she ate there. "I should have left him my food." But she was hungry and the burger, potato salad and chocolate cupcakes might make her feel better once she got home.

Once back in her apartment, Abby sat by the window, her favorite spot to eat, and tried to enjoy her lunch. But the image of Nate and how he was when she'd left kept filling her mind, and it irritated her. What happened in her past was for her and her alone. She didn't have to tell him or anybody why she'd wanted the teaching job here in New Berne. It wasn't as if she would have been hired in New Wilmington. If she'd stayed in the vicinity of her family, she'd have suffered from being constantly faced with her sister and ex-betrothed's betrayal…and the way her parents seemed fine with it.

Tears filled her eyes and she blinked to clear them. She was in a lovely place with a job she'd always wanted. If she had to avoid Nate Hostetler to be happy, she would.

Across the room on the counter near the door sat her sister and Peter's wedding invitation. She stood and went to get it. A shaft of pain ran through her as she read the words that she'd expected to one day belong on an invitation to her and Peter's union. Enough! She wasn't going to allow them to hurt her anymore. She would continue with her life here and forget about everything that had happened before she'd left her hometown. New Berne would be her home now, and she would grab hold of any happiness she could find here.

She'd give herself one day off before she returned to the school to finish the walls and then check at the progress on the cottage—her soon-to-be new home. Abby decided she would ignore the man doing the work there and go whenever she wanted whether he liked it or not. She wouldn't allow anyone, especially Nathaniel Hostetler, to ruin her fresh start.

* * *

Nate sat at the picnic table and closed his eyes. He'd been a fool asking Abby personal questions that she clearly hadn't wanted to answer. He'd allowed his bad experience with Emily to cloud his judgment. Abby was a newcomer here. He had no right to her thoughts or her history.

He ate his lunch, then took his root beer to the cottage to check on the drying progress of the spackle. It looked smooth and ready for the next step. Yet as Nate started to sand it, his mind remained on Abby Yost. In the end, he went home early, his head still full of thoughts of Abby. His guilt about his behavior made getting a good sleep that night difficult.

When he returned to work the next day, he couldn't help but wonder if Abby would stay away or return to finish what she'd started—cleaning the schoolhouse's walls. The woman never showed, and his guilt intensified.

The following day, at nine-thirty, Nate was inside the house with the windows open, painting the front room, when he heard a horse-drawn vehicle on the lane. He peeked out through the cottage window, watching as Abby tied up her horse and went into the school. He didn't rush out to talk with her; he didn't want to cause her to leave. Nate waited a few minutes, picked up the two coffees he'd purchased a little while ago as an apology and headed to the school.

As he approached, a second buggy drove onto the lane. It wasn't from Lancaster County, as it was brown. The buggies in New Berne were gray. He stood back and watched as a woman got out, leaving the male driver. Nate headed in her direction.

"Can I help you?" Nate eyed her curiously. She was attractive enough physically, with blond hair and blue eyes, but there was a snooty air about her as she studied him. He got the impression that she felt she was better than him.

She nodded. "I'm looking for Abigail Yost. I understand she will be working here."

"*Ja*, she will be." His gaze narrowed. He didn't like it when she studied the schoolhouse as if disgusted by it. "May I ask what you want with her?"

The woman sniffed and seemed to stand taller. "I need to talk with her. I'm her *schweschter*." She seemed to note the two coffees in his hand. "Well, is she here?" the woman asked impatiently.

He stiffened at her attitude. "She's in the *schulehaus*."

"Why didn't you say so?" She spun and walked away. The door was open and she vanished inside.

Nate followed and set down the coffee near the brick exterior he'd worked on yesterday. He took a moment to check on the repair work he'd done, pleased with how nice it looked. He wanted to go in after the stranger, but he didn't want to barge in while Abby talked with her sister. The windows were open, and he vaguely heard conversation from inside the school. When the sound of raised voices reached him, he grew concerned and peeked through the window screen. He saw the newcomer angrily giving Abby a piece of her mind before throwing something on the desk as she made mention of a wedding. Abby spoke too softly for him to hear, but whatever she said increased the other woman's anger.

"You will be there!" the woman said in a demanding voice.

"Why?" Abby's response was louder this time. "Why do you need me?"

"Because it's expected. Because we're family, and it

would lead to talk if you don't come!" She stomped her foot. "You will not embarrass us by not attending!"

Her angry outburst upset Nate. Abby's face was pale as she stared at her sister. He moved around to the door and was about to intervene when the male driver in the buggy got out and headed toward the school. Nate stayed back to see what would happen.

Abby's sister exited the building, saw the man and started to sob before she threw herself into his arms. "She's being awful again, Peter!"

As the man tried to calm her sister, Abby called out, "I'll be there."

The couple didn't acknowledge her as they got into their buggy and left.

Frowning, Nate went inside and his heart broke when he caught Abby crying. She stood with her hands on the desktop, bent over. "Abby…"

She gasped and looked up. "Nate." Abby turned away to wipe her eyes. When she'd calmed, she faced him again. "Sorry. I got something in my eye."

He softened his expression as he approached and handed her the coffee. "It should still be hot."

Some of her spunk returned as she raised her eyebrows. "How did you know I'd be here today?"

"I didn't," he admitted with a smile. "I bought you a coffee yesterday but you didn't come." He paused to draw a calming breath. "It's my apology for being rude."

Her mouth started to curve. *"Danki."* She took a sip. "Just the way I like it."

"And the way I drink it, too." He grew serious as he regarded her. "Was that obnoxious woman really your sister?"

Abby blinked and then laughed outright. "Obnoxious, huh?" He nodded. *"Ja,* that was my sister, Clara. And the man was her fiancé, Peter Graber." She picked up a paper from the desk. "They wanted to make sure I had this." She sighed as she threw it down again. "It's their wedding invitation. The second one I received. They are going to marry in late July, sooner than they'd first planned. The original invitation put their wedding at the end of August."

"Why was she yelling?" he asked, keeping his voice soft.

"I don't want to go," she said weakly as she averted her glance.

"Why not?" He grew concerned as he studied her.

"Peter was my betrothed first." She refused to meet his gaze as she continued. "We were together for six months before he discarded me to be with Clara." She blinked back tears. "I discovered they'd been seeing each other in secret."

Nate's eyes widened. "Your *schweschter* stole your man?" He was surprised by the revelation that she'd endured heartbreak and rejection, like he'd suffered.

Abby must have heard something in his tone that gave away his shock. "*Ja.* Apparently, he decided that he was in love with Clara."

"Let's sit at the picnic table," he suggested. Fresh air would help her right now. "We can drink our coffees there."

She seemed to hesitate for a moment before she nodded and trailed behind him as he left the building and took a seat where they'd sat previously, across from each other.

"I know how you feel," Nate said after a moment of silence. "I was courting a woman named Emily. I thought we were in love, but she refused to marry me, saying she couldn't see herself married to a farmer. She accepted a job offer out of state. I heard she met and married someone only a few months after she left."

Abby's features softened with understanding. "You do understand."

He inclined his head. "Did I hear you agree to attend their wedding?"

"*Ja*, I had to." She sighed. "Yet, it doesn't seem to matter. I know the first thing Clara will do when she gets home is complain to my parents."

"About what?" Nate watched many changes in her expression before the last one—resignation.

"That I'm not understanding enough. That I'm being selfish and inconsiderate for saying I don't want to come."

"But I can't imagine anyone would expect you to go to the trouble and expense of returning home to witness a wedding that's sure to be upsetting for you." It seemed obvious to Nate that Clara would be the cruel one if she insisted that Abby attend. Surely their parents would see it the same way.

Abby shrugged. "My parents have always favored Clara. They didn't think it was a big deal when Peter decided he wanted her instead of me." She paused to sip from her coffee. "I was supposed to accept it and move on quickly."

Nate scowled. "Surely not."

"*Ja*, it's true." Abby gave him a wry smile. "They are already angry with me because I dared to accept a teaching position away from home when I should have stayed and helped with their wedding plans." She rubbed her cheek. "I have always wanted a teaching job. I used to volunteer at the local *schule*. My parents didn't like it. When I wasn't making money at my other jobs outside the home, they wanted me to work in the *haus*. But I loved being with the children, even though I was an assistant more than a teacher since I couldn't be there all the time." She looked alarmed by her admission. "I'll be a *gut* teacher, Nate. I won't let anyone down."

He smiled. "I know you won't."

She raised her hand and let it fall. "Now I have to go to this wedding," she said. "And it will be embarrassing since everyone there knows my beau wanted my sister more than me."

After drinking from his coffee, he set down his cup and eyed her thoughtfully. There was a way he could help her but only if she agreed to his crazy idea. She'd suffered heartbreak, and he knew all about it with Emily. Because he understood, he felt drawn to do what he could for her.

"What?" she asked when he continued to stare at her. "Do I have something on my nose?"

"Nay," he said with laughter. "I think I can help with your wedding problem."

She gazed at him with her pretty, green eyes. "How?"

"I'll go to the wedding with you. We can pretend to be newly engaged sweethearts. Then no one will pity you for losing Peter. We can show everyone—your parents and sister with her fiancé included—that you have moved on... with me." He watched for her reaction as he continued to drink his coffee.

Abby got up and hugged herself with her arms. She walked away from the picnic table a few steps, then stopped and met his gaze. "I don't know..."

Nate studied her with warmth. "It will be fine. You shouldn't have to attend alone."

"You'd do that? For me?" Her voice was soft and her expression hopeful as she returned to the picnic table and sat down.

"Ja." He took his last swallow and set down his cup. He had left his hat in the cottage, and he ran his hand nervously through his hair. "So, what do you say? Shall we be pretend sweethearts before becoming betrothed? Of course, we'll need to convince the New Berne community first that

we're a couple, especially since we will be going on a trip together." He waited for her response, hoping she'd say yes.

Abby looked unsure. "Nate, I don't know. It seems a lot to ask of you."

He smiled. "You haven't asked. I'm offering." It would be good for him, too, if their community realized that he'd moved on from Emily. Everyone had known the woman he loved had left him. He wasn't in love with her after what had happened, but it was hard to make others understand that he wasn't still pining for her. "Well? What do you say?"

"Okey." Her simple answer was the one he'd been hoping for, causing him to grin.

"How long of a ride is it to New Wilmington? That's where the wedding will be, *ja*?" He stretched his arms backward to relieve tense muscles from the construction work he'd been doing.

"About five hours by bus," she said. "A lot longer by buggy, of course."

Nate gaped at her for a moment. "Did Clara and Peter drive all the way here by buggy?"

She chuckled as if she found his reaction amusing. "You don't know my *schweschter*. Clara always gets what she wants. And I have a feeling they've been staying with friends and family before they got here. And I'm sure they'll be staying overnight at two separate places on the way home. She loves to brag about her fiancé to anyone who will listen. Another person to impress."

"I wasn't impressed by her," he mumbled beneath his breath, but she heard him.

Abby's grin seemed wider than Preacher Jonas's land acreage. "So, what's the plan? What should we do first?"

"We'll spend more time together at the *schule* and cottage for a start. And we can eat together at Fannie's Luncheonette and discuss our plan so we can get to know one another better." He gestured toward her cup. "Are you done?"

She handed it to him. "So that's all we have to do?"

He opened the lids and stacked one cup into the other one. "Our fellow community members will do the rest. We have quite a few here who love to natter." He stood and then helped her rise. "When did you say the wedding was?"

"July. I have an invitation inside on the desk you can have."

He stilled. "I'm sorry about what I said the other day."

"It's *okey*." She went into the school with him following her.

"It's not. You didn't deserve it." He touched her shoulder, drawing her gaze. "Forgive me?"

She nodded and smiled at him. "Here's the invitation." She handed it to him.

He could feel Abby studying him as he read it. He met her gaze and saw the worry in her expression.

"Do you think this plan of yours will work? Be honest." She shifted as he studied the invitation in his hand.

"*Ja*, it will work," he told her confidently, determined that they'd pull it off without any problems. He'd only met Abby a few days ago, but he knew all too well how heartbreak could follow a person for a long time. If he could help her move on and help her save face in front of her family and friends, he was only too happy to do it.

Chapter Six

Abby stood at the doorway to the dining room, peeking inside to see Nate seated at a table, waiting for her. This morning, as part of their plan for their fake relationship, they would be eating breakfast together at Fannie's. When Linda suddenly came up behind her with a coffeepot, she gasped.

"*Gut mariga*, Abby," the young woman said. "Ready for breakfast?"

Abby nodded. "I'm meeting Nate."

"*Ja.* He told me. Coffee?" Linda held up the pot.

"I'd love some. *Danki.*" Her heart thundered in her chest as Abby followed Linda into the dining room. Nate looked up as Linda poured him a cup of coffee, then his gaze sought out hers after the server filled a second mug for Abby. He didn't smile, but there was a warmth and an intensity in his brown eyes that she felt right down to her toes. Linda promised to return for their order as Abby pulled out a chair across from him.

It was only after the other woman left that Nate's expression softened and he smiled at her. "*Hallo*, Abby. Did you sleep well?"

Abby bit her lip, unsure how to answer. "I—ah—"

"You were worried about this morning and how this

fake courtship will work." He had lowered his tone so only Abby could hear him, although there were no other customers in the room.

She blushed. "*Ja.* I slept a little but mostly I was awake."

"Funny," he said softly. "I slept fine. Better than I have in a long time."

Abby felt an odd sensation along her skin. "You did?"

Nate nodded. "Try not to worry. We'll figure this out. *Okey?*"

"*Okey.*" Convinced by his assurance, Abby managed a smile.

It was strange how a few words from this man could make her muscles relax and her nervousness ease. She gave him a nod and took her cue from him to have a normal conversation. "What are you planning to work on today? The *haus* or the *schule*?" After he gestured for her to go first, she stirred milk and sugar into her coffee, then passed them to him.

"I have work to do in both places, but I thought I take off just for today." He smiled as he added the same to his mug. "I need to paint rooms in the cottage but I need to pick up more paint. Once I'm done with the cottage, I'll finish repairs to the outside of the *schule* building."

"Is there anything I can do to help?" She took a sip from her cup.

"You can come to the cottage so I can show you what's been done. Since you'll be living there, I want to discuss a few things to make sure that you're happy with the layout in the kitchen and bathroom." Nate leaned back as Linda returned to take their orders. They both spoke at the same time as each ordered the omelet special with bacon and home fries.

Abby chuckled as Linda left. "We like the same coffee and apparently we both like the same type of omelets and sides."

Nate nodded. "The food here is *wunderbor*. You won't be disappointed."

"I haven't been. Fannie is a fine cook." She sighed. "I wish I'd learned to cook more than a few breakfast items." Abby smiled. "Fannie promised to teach me after I begin to pitch in whenever she's short-staffed."

"That's nice of you." He stared at her as if memorizing her features.

She shifted uncomfortably under his regard. "I'm the one getting the better end of the deal."

Nate leaned forward, and she noted his unique scent. "So, tell me more about you. We'll need to know a great deal about each other to make our relationship appear authentic."

Abby sighed. "I think you know more about me than I do you."

"We'll get to me. Tell me about growing up in New Wilmington." The front door to the luncheonette opened, drawing their attention as customers entered—a family of four. Coming into the room with her and Nate's food, Linda smiled at the newcomers and invited them to sit wherever they wanted. The family chose to sit on the other side of the room, for which Abby was grateful. She didn't want anyone eavesdropping on her and Nate's conversation.

Abby barely noticed that Linda had set down their food in front of them. After the server left, she once again had Nate's full attention. "New Wilmington is a pretty area," she began. "There is a lot of beautiful farmland outside of town." She took a sip of coffee. "I imagine it gets much colder during the winter there than here in New Berne since it's located further north."

Nate shrugged. "It gets cold here, too. We get a lot of snow, so I'll let you be the judge of our winter weather."

She watched as he ate some of his omelet and she took a bite of hers. It was delicious. Then she sampled a forkful of home fries, which had been cooked perfectly.

"What did you do back home?" He smiled. "Besides help out in the classroom."

"I cleaned our *haus*, worked in a bakery and also had a job in the general store." She hated confessing that she had to work when her sister hadn't, so she didn't mention that Clara had never held a job.

"How many siblings do you have?" He nibbled on a piece of bacon.

"Just my *schweschter*, Clara." Abby stared at her plate, anticipating and worrying about his next question.

"Just the two of you? I have two *bruders*. Aaron, who used to live here before he took a position with a large Indiana construction company and an older *bruder*, Samuel who married when Aaron and I were children, a year after our *eldre* died. Sam looked after us until our *grossmammi* took Aaron and me in. Then Sam and Miriam got married and moved to be closer to Miriam's family in Ohio."

Abby felt compassion as she studied him. "How old were you when your *mam* and *dat* passed?"

A hint of sadness entered his expression. "I was ten and Aaron twelve." He hesitated. "Sam was nineteen." He met her gaze, his brown eyes glistening.

"So young," she murmured, feeling sorrow for the little boy Nate had been. She touched his shoulder. "How awful."

"*Ja*, it was a terrible time for us. *Mam* and *Dat* died in a car crash while shopping in another state. They'd left us at home since Sam was old enough to watch us." From his expression, it was clear to Abby that he still felt the shock and horror of the day he'd received the news of his parents' deaths.

"Were they *gut eldre*?" she asked softly.

"They were strict, but we never doubted how much they loved us." He seemed lost in thought for a moment before he pulled himself out enough to smile at her.

"How long has it been since you've seen Sam?"

"Close to thirteen years now."

The front door opened again, and Abby watched as another group entered the room and took seats too close to theirs for a quiet conversation. She was ready to leave but neither one of them had eaten much of their breakfast.

"Why don't we get food containers and coffee to go and we can continue this conversation near the *schule*," Nate suggested as if he'd read her mind.

When Linda came back into the room, Nate waved her over and told her what they wanted. She left to get their boxes and cups of fresh coffee to go. She returned and set them down.

"May I have the bill?" Abby asked, determined to pay for their meal.

"Nay," Linda said. "Fannie said there is no charge for you and Nate."

"But—"

Nate frowned. "I'll pay for breakfast."

"Nay. The two of you are important to this community and are doing us a service. If you don't like it, I suggest you speak to Fannie herself. But Fannie isn't in right now, so you'll have to wait until she is available." She grinned. "And if you think I'm stubborn, wait until you talk with her."

"Ach, I will," Nate said with authority.

Linda only chuckled. "Have a lovely day! Come back

and see us again." Then she went to take orders from the group who had come in last.

It was raining as they opened the restaurant's back door. Nate looked toward the barn where Abby's pony cart was kept and then at his buggy parked closer to the building. "Why don't you ride with me? I can bring you back later."

The sky had been clear when he'd arrived but now it was dark as if the rain would continue for some time.

Abby glanced toward the horizon. "Are you sure? I can stop by another day."

He shook his head. "I'd like to talk with you today." Nate gauged the distance they'd have to run as the rain picked up. "Wait here. I'll get the buggy and bring it closer to you."

"I don't mind a little rain," she said as she studied his vehicle across the distance.

"It's up to you, but I'm happy to keep you and our breakfast from getting wet." He handed her his cup along with the food containers, and he was pleased how easily she managed to shift items in her hands to accommodate all of them. "I'll be right back."

She waited in the doorway while he ran to the vehicle, climbed inside, turned on the battery-run windshield wipers and then steered the horse-drawn vehicle closer to Abby. Nate leaned across to accept the food containers from her first and set them on the back seat floor. Then he reached for the coffee cups and set them in the cup holders attached to the front of the buggy. Abby got in quickly and shut the door before she grinned at him.

"Nice day for a ride, *ja*?" Her green eyes sparkled as he held her gaze.

He laughed. Her lightheartedness warmed him as he

pulled away and made a right onto the road that led to the school and cottage property. "It is," he agreed.

He could feel her eyes settle on him before she studied the inside of his buggy. "Nice cup holders and dash," she commented.

"Aaron and I bought it after our construction business became successful. We traded in our *grosseldre*'s buggy for a better model."

The swish-swish of the windshields was comforting and made it easier for Nate to see through the pouring rain.

"Maybe we should have stayed at Fannie's," Abby said after a rumble of thunder rent the air.

Nate shook his head with a smile. "We'll be fine in the cottage. I even brought a couple of folding chairs there the other day."

Another clap of thunder. A much louder one. He felt Abby nearly jump in her seat at the sound. *"Ach,"* she murmured. "It's getting harder to see. Do you think we should pull over?"

Nate bent his head to get a better look at the sky through the windshield. "You're right—we should stop for a while." He noted where they were and soon put on the blinker before he turned into a parking lot behind a store. After he drove to the back of the building, he pulled into an open barn they had for their Amish customers. "I'm going to check on Martin."

"Martin?" she asked, hugging herself as a flash of lightning lit up the barn, followed by a thunder boom.

"My horse." Nate got out of his buggy and moved toward Martin. The gelding didn't seem frightened. Still, he murmured to the animal softly as he ran a hand over its withers soothingly.

He went to Abby's side and she rolled down the window.

"Would you hand me the towel under your seat?" She bent to retrieve it, then handed it him, and he ran the towel over the horse to remove as much of the wetness as he could.

Nate climbed back into the driver's seat and smiled. "Want to finish our breakfast? We have all the comforts of home here. No sense waiting for the rain to stop so we can get to the cottage. Let's eat."

Abby blinked at his teasing and grinned. *"Okey."*

He reached over the back to grab the food boxes on the floor, which brought him closer to Abby. Facing the front again, he read the names Linda had written on the boxes and handed Abby hers.

The vehicle filled with the scent of eggs, potatoes and bacon. They had eaten little before they left, so they tucked into their meal with murmurs of appreciation between bites. Nate sensed when Abby relaxed, intent on her food.

They were quiet as they ate until he broke the silence. "Tell me more about yourself. You said you worked in a bakery."

Abby nodded. *"Ja.* I mostly worked the counter, serving customers, but I did learn to make some things like muffins and cupcakes. But that's all I know how to bake."

Nate smiled. "I bet they were delicious."

She shrugged. "They were *okey.* My first attempt wasn't so *gut,* but the owner gave me another chance." She grinned. "Those were delicious."

He laughed, charmed by her good humor and willingness to poke gentle fun at herself.

They finished their breakfast and chatted. The time passed quickly as they sat in the buggy while the storm raged outside. Soon, the rain stopped and the sun peeked out for a moment from behind dark clouds.

"I guess we can head to the cottage now," Nate said as

he took her empty container and tucked it with his on the floor behind their seat. He took one last sip from his coffee to hold him over until they reached the teacher's house. He studied her and saw her smiling as she gazed at him while she drank from her cup.

He concentrated on getting on the road again, his thoughts on Abby beside him. It would be no hardship to pretend to have a relationship with this woman. At the same time, though, their agreement was temporary only and he was grateful for that. They could be friends but nothing more. He was just doing Abby a favor, and that was all there was to it.

Chapter Seven

The rain was spritzing by the time Nate pulled his buggy behind the cottage and tied up Martin to the post there. As she climbed down from the vehicle, Abby looked at the back of the house with excitement. This would be her home come late August or early September. She couldn't wait to move in and have the freedom to do whatever she wanted not what her parents had insisted she do.

She walked toward the back door and waited for Nate to unlock it before she preceded him inside. It had been over a week since she'd stopped in to see it last.

Abby gasped with pleasure. Sheetrock usually made a room look smaller, but this one seemed much larger than she'd expected. "Nate, it looks *wunderbor*! This will be the kitchen area, *ja*?" There was a window along one wall that looked as if it belonged above the sink.

"*Ja*, I thought you might like it." He smiled, looking pleased with her reaction. "Let me tell you what I was thinking for the layout of the cabinets, stove and refrigerator." He moved toward the largest space in the corner of the room. "Better yet, why don't you tell me where you want them?"

"I'd be happy with anything," she said, enthusiastic with what she'd seen of the house so far. She met his gaze. His eyes were brown with a hint of gold in them, and they regarded her with warmth. She loved the way his gaze lit up whenever something gave him pleasure. "Would you tell me what your plans are?" Her anticipation built when she saw him nod.

"I'd put the cabinets in this space with the sink under the window," he said, gesturing toward the area she'd first noticed when she came in. He blinked as he looked at her. "Something wrong?" he asked when she studied her intently.

"Nay." She smiled. "It's just that... I thought the same thing. That window is a *wunderbor* place to put the sink," she admitted, which made him grin. "Please...go on."

"The countertop with wall and base cabinets will go along here and there." Nate gestured toward the larger corner.

It sounded perfect, she mused. Abby hid her delight as he continued to explain where the stove and refrigerator could be set.

"A pantry closet would fit right there," he continued and then explained the measurements and about the type of wood—oak—that would be used for the cabinetry.

Abby listened with pleasure to the deep voice of the man who was making her future a reality. Lost in her thoughts, she began to picture cups and glasses in one wall unit with dishes in another.

"Abby?"

"Ja?" Her name on his lips shook her from her thoughts about making the cottage her home.

He frowned. "What do you think about the layout?"

Abby beamed at him. "I love it. I love absolutely everything you described." She would live in a house of her own, with the job she'd always wanted. She felt like she'd been flooded with blessings.

His brow cleared and Nate returned her grin. "*Gut, gut.* Would you like to see the rest of the *haus*?"

Her vigorous nod made him laugh.

"Let's me show you the bathroom, living and bedroom areas." He led the way and Abby automatically followed, eager to see the rest of the cottage. "All the rooms will be white, of course."

Abby nodded. "Of course." Amish families tended to have white walls in their homes, although she supposed there might be one or two who were daring enough to use color.

"As soon as the painting's done, the floors over this sub-floor will go in and shortly afterward the furniture will arrive."

She blinked, having forgotten about furniture. "I don't have to buy my own?"

Nate just looked at her. "Are you seriously asking me that? You're going to be the new teacher. Members of our church community are honored to be able to make sure you have everything you need."

"I… I guess I should have known but…" No one had done much of anything for her during her life. Everything that was happening in New Berne was turning out to be wonderful, and she offered up a prayer of thanks to the Lord for this town and these people.

Thunder in the distance warned of another impending storm. A flash of lightning drew Abby to the window just as the dark clouds released a heavy downpour. As she watched, the landscape outside faded under the water streaming down the glass windowpane.

Nate joined her there, and she became overly aware of his nearness…his clean masculine scent. "We should wait this out before we head back to Fannie's, don't you think?" he asked, his voice a deep male rumble near her right ear.

Abby turned and found him close...extremely close. "What about your horse?"

"Martin will be *oll recht*." He went into the other room, and Abby followed him, stopping on the threshold of the open doorway as he peeked through the kitchen window to check on his gelding. "I need to build you a barn. You'll need shelter for your horse and buggy."

A flash of lightning lit up the room, startling Abby. "You could bring him inside," she offered. "I don't mind. I'm sure it will be *okey*."

Nate shook his head. "I don't know."

"What if we bring him into the *schule*?" she suggested.

"*Nay*. He's used to bad weather." Nate joined her at the door. A gust of wind blew inside the cottage, forcing rain inside. "We'd better shut the door."

"Isn't it dangerous under that tree?" Damp, Abby felt a chill and hugged herself with her arms.

"Not always." His smile reassured her. "The storm shouldn't last long. Let's sit down for a while." Nate opened a folding chair and gestured for Abby to sit. Then he sat in the other chair.

"Let's talk about the first step in our fake courtship." He smiled at her. "Starting slow will be more convincing and believable to our church community."

"What should we do?" she asked, turning in her chair to get more comfortable.

"Sunday service? We'll appear to talk with each other... but not too much. Go ahead and spend time meeting other church members—it's what everyone will expect, and they all want to meet you." He took off his hat and ran fingers through his brown locks. "If some other fellow shows too much interest in you, I'll be sure to join the two of you and pretend to be jealous. I wouldn't want you to fall for any other eligible bachelors in New Berne." He was grinning when their gazes met.

His explanation caused her to feel a little flutter inside. She knew he was teasing her, but the thought of him wanting to ward off other suitors pleased her...even it wasn't real.

"And after Sunday?" Abby wondered what was next.

"Will you be helping Fannie out next week?" he asked, his gaze intent.

"Maybe. I told her I'd help if she needs me. I can let you know if I'll be working." Abby tucked a tiny, escaped tendril of golden blond hair back under her *kapp*.

"Gut," he said. "I'll talk with you about it on Sunday."

They sat in silence for a moment before a distant roll of thunder alerted them that the storm had passed on.

Nate stood up. "I guess we should head back." He held out his hand and she accepted his help to rise. His fingers felt warm and wonderful against hers.

They exited the house the same way they had come in. Nate reached his buggy first and grabbed another towel from inside, which he rubbed along the horse. Murmuring to the animal, he dried Martin and then tossed the cloth back into the rear of the buggy.

Next, he opened the door for Abby and helped her climb in. Surprised by how considerate he was, she sat and waited for him to get in on the other side, her heart humming happily in her chest.

Being this close to Nate made it difficult for her to think and breathe evenly, but she did. The man had agreed to help her out, but she couldn't forget that it was nothing more than pretend.

As he drove her back to her apartment, Abby studied the landscape through the side window. The grass and trees looked greener. They passed farmland and she noted the height of the corn planted in the spring and she recognized the soybean plants that sprouted from the ground, along with the acreage that had been seeded with hay.

"You're quiet," Nate murmured, drawing her attention.

She met his gaze and smiled. "I'm noticing how the rain has affected the land. Everything is nice and green."

Although his attention was back on the road in front of them, she noted the slight upward curve of his lips. "You're *recht*."

Abby recalled Fannie mentioned that Nate had made a sacrifice to work on the cottage and school. Dare she ask him? She bit her lip and decided to go for it. "Nate?"

"Hmm?" He flipped on a blinker and made the turn onto another road.

"May I ask you something? And if it's too personal, you don't have to tell me." She saw him stiffen.

"You can ask," he said, "but I may not answer."

"Fair enough," she murmured, studying him as he drove. The man was most certainly handsome—not that she was supposed to be noticing that.

He shot her a quick glance. "Ask me, then."

"Someone mentioned that it was a sacrifice for you to agree to work on the cottage and *schule*. May I ask what it was you sacrificed?"

To her surprise, he chuckled. "It was not a true sacrifice," he said after he'd flashed a smile at her. "I simply put off something I wanted to do."

"Would you mind telling me what it is?" She wanted to know, wanted to understand him better.

"I've worked for Jonas on his dairy farm for over three

years now. My end goal is to raise dairy cows of my own."
He grew quiet and seemed reflective for a minute. "I finally
have enough money to make a deposit on farm property."

"I see," she said, although she didn't. "Won't your farm
compete with the preacher's?"

"Nay," he said with a glance in her direction. "Jonas
can't fulfill all the needs of our community. When he first
hired me, he said that when I was ready to branch out, he'd
give me a cow or two to start."

"Jonas seems like a *gut* man." She noticed a dairy farm
coming up on the right side of the road. "Is that his?"

"Ja. And you're right that he's a *gut* man. He's generous
too. I've been fortunate to be working for him." Something
in his tone had her studying his profile. She was relieved
to see good humor in his expression. "I'm working on your
cottage and *schule* because of Jonas." Nate laughed. "The
man could convince anyone to do anything. There was no
way I could turn him down."

"I'm sure Jonas thinks you're the best man for the job,"
she offered softly.

"Ach, for sure and for certain." He turned on the blinker
and it was then that Abby noticed that they were back at
Fannie's Luncheonette and her apartment upstairs.

He drove around to the back of the building and tied up
his horse. To Abby's surprise, he got out when she did. "I
thought I'd buy lunch while I'm here to bring home with
me for later."

Abby nodded, "You know they're not going to let you
pay, don't you?"

Nate froze in his tracks. "I… I forgot, I guess." He
scowled but then continued inside the back door,
which was open this time of day. "If she won't let me pay,
then I'll leave and go over to Kings."

She giggled. Abby couldn't help herself. He looked at her as if there was something wrong with her. "I think you're an honorable man, Nate Hostetler."

His expression softened. "That's kind of you to say, but you should know that I'm also stubborn...to a fault."

Abby studied his handsome face. "I don't mind stubborn. The only fault that would truly bother me would be if you were dishonest. But you would be honest with me, wouldn't you? I need to know that I can trust you during our arrangement."

"You can trust that I'll be honest and up-front with you," he said, and she could tell he meant it.

Abby was grinning as she preceded him down the hall.

Fannie came out of the kitchen. "Abby." Her gaze then settled on Nate. "Nathaniel. How is the cottage coming along?"

"It's coming along fine," he said with a slight smile.

"*Gut, gut.* I'm glad," Fannie said. She looked from him to Abby. "Are you looking for lunch?"

Nate nodded. "But if you won't let me pay for it, I'll go to Kings instead."

Abby couldn't keep the wide smile off her face. Fannie met her gaze and grinned back at her.

"Fine, then," Fannie said. "I'll let you pay this time. What will you have?"

His order was lost on Abby who headed toward the stairs. "*Danki* for showing me the cottage today, Nate," she said sincerely. "I enjoyed seeing all you've done."

He gave her a nod. "You're *willkomm.*"

As she left, she could feel his eyes on her until she started up the steps.

She kind of liked Nate. On the one hand, it would make it easier to pretend to be courting him. But on the other, she would need to be careful not to get carried away. The last thing she needed was to complicate her life by falling for the man. After her painful parting with Peter, who had committed to a future with her, Abby knew she needed to beware of letting another man into her life and her heart. Yet, Nate continued to remain in her thoughts more than he should.

Chapter Eight

Abby didn't know what to do with herself. She was used to working both at home and at her paying jobs back in New Wilmington. As grueling as that workload had been, it had meant that she'd always had something to do. Being idle now felt strange and unnatural. She longed to plan her lessons for the new school year, but the textbooks for each grade level hadn't arrived yet. Today she wondered if she could convince Fannie to allow her to help in the restaurant. Maybe she could do a few simple things before Fannie and her staff came in.

Saturday morning Fannie's was only open during the breakfast hours from 8 a.m. until 11. It was too early for food prep, which was why Fannie wasn't in yet. Abby wandered into the dining room to check that each table had full settings: place mats, utensils rolled inside napkins, and coffee cups turned upside down. She took note of a few missing items and then retrieved them from the kitchen. Thanks to Fannie and her insistence that she use the kitchen whatever she wanted, Abby knew where everything was. She grabbed coffee mugs and put them at each table settings then added utensils and napkins where they were missing.

After the dining room was ready for opening, Abby hurried to eat breakfast. The last thing she wanted was to be in

Fannie's way when the young woman came in to prepare food. After deciding on a sweet muffin with a cup of tea, she stood at the kitchen worktable to enjoy them. As she was finishing her breakfast, she heard the back door open and Fannie's voice on the phone.

"It's fine, Linda," Fannie said. "I understand. You certainly can't come in if you're sick." There was a pause as if she was listening. "Don't worry. I'll manage. Stay home and rest. I'll check in with you later, *ja*?"

Fannie entered the kitchen and grabbed her apron on the right side of the door. When she turned, she turned to see Abby. *"Gut mariga!"*

"Gut mariga. You looked tired," Abby said. The woman was pregnant, and while she was usually full of energy, today it looked as if she was feeling the strain. "I didn't mean to overhear, but I can help you today if you'd like."

Fannie blinked. "You can?"

Abby bobbed her head. *"Ja,* I'm used to working, and I need something to do. I already checked the dining room and put out coffee mugs, and any missing utensils and napkins in the place settings."

"Danki." Fannie appeared pleased with Abby's help. "We didn't get a chance to check yesterday. It was a busy day, and I was tired. I'd already sent Linda home because she didn't feel well."

"I can serve," she told her. "And bus tables. And if you tell me what to do, I can help in the kitchen, too."

"Are you sure?" Fannie absently rubbed her rounded belly as if trying to relieve discomfort.

Abby smiled. "For sure and for certain." She grabbed another full apron from the hook by the door and put it on, tying it at her neck and waist. Approaching Fannie, she smiled. "I honestly will be glad to do what I can. I'm not used to doing nothing. Please let me be here for you like you've been for me."

Fannie nodded. "You are a lifesaver," she murmured.

"*Nay*, you are...for me." She joined Fannie at the work-table and picked up her empty teacup before putting it in the commercial dishwasher. "What would you like me to do first?"

Her friend pulled a chair out from the wall and sat down. "I'm sorry. I'm feeling these babies today."

Abby gaped at her. "Babies?"

Fannie grinned. "*Ja*, David and I are having twins."

"Congratulations!" She grinned even as she wondered how Fannie would manage two newborns here and at home after she gave birth. "I'm happy for you."

"Danki." Fannie's blue eyes lit up with happiness. "We feel blessed and thankful."

Abby longed for a husband and family of her own. But it appeared the Lord must have other plans for her. At least she would be able to take joy in teaching the children of others.

"What are the specials for the day?" Abby asked, wondering where she should start.

"Griddle corn cakes and fruit-baked oatmeal," Fannie told her. "And of course, we have eggs, sausage or bacon with home fries and toast for those who prefer a standard breakfast." She began to take out the ingredients. "We'll need to prepare the oatmeal with fruit first since it has to bake for thirty-five to forty minutes."

Fannie continued to instruct her on what to do. Abby beamed at her after she placed the oatmeal bars into the oven.

"I know how to make eggs and breakfast meats," Abby said. That was one meal she'd perfected because of her mother's poor attempts to cook it. "I'm sure I can handle making pancakes."

"*Wunderbor!*" her friend exclaimed. "*Gut* to know."

Soon the first customers entered the dining room, and Abby explained the specials of the day, took their orders and served their coffees. She was able to keep up with the flow of people who came to dine.

Later that morning the door opened and an Amish couple entered. The man took off his wide-brimmed, black-banded straw hat to reveal a handsome face under a cap of dark hair. He led his pregnant wife, a blonde with blue eyes, to a table near the side window of the room. Abby waited for them to be seated before she approached,

She smiled at them. "*Hallo*, my name is Abby, and I'll be taking care of you today. Would you like coffee?"

"*Ia, danki,*" he said. "Em?"

The woman lay her hands on her big belly. "Do you have decaf?"

"We do." Abby smiled. "The specials today are baked fruit oatmeal and griddle corn cakes. I'll give you time to look over the menu." She flipped their cups right side up, ready to be filled.

Abby went to the kitchen for the coffee and then returned to the dining room. She heard whispers from another table as she slowly approached the couple's table with a pot in each hand.

"Isn't that Emily Fisher?" an older Amish woman murmured to her friend.

"She must be back to see her *bruder*," her friend replied softly. "It's about time she showed up again. The girl has been gone a long time."

"I heard someone whispering to her friend about the woman who just came in with her husband," Abby told

Fannie as she returned the kitchen. "Her name is Emily Fisher. Do you know her?" Could this be the girl who had broken Nate's heart? He had said that her name was Emily.

"Emily's here?" Fannie brightened. "She must be in town to see Gabriel. I'll go and say a quick *hallo*." She seemed eager to see the woman as she hurried toward the dining room. Abby followed her in with the coffeepots—one decaf and one regular.

"Emily Fisher!" Fannie greeted as she reached the table. "Are you here to catch up with your *bruder*?"

"Fannie! It's *gut* to see you!" Emily piped up. "*Ja*, we're here to visit Gabriel." She smiled at the man across from her. "This is my husband, Abraham Burkholder. Abraham, this is Fannie Miller. She owns this fine establishment."

"Fannie Troyer," Fannie said with a grin. "I married David Troyer. I see you're about to have a little one. I'll soon have three with my *dochter* Rose." She patted her stomach. "Twins!"

"Three children!" Emily grinned. "I have been away a long time."

Abby filled Abraham's coffee cup and then Emily's. She was still wondering if this was Nate's Emily. If so, did he know she was back in town? Would he be upset that she was here? Too many questions ran through her mind as she brought the coffeepots to the kitchen. When she came back into the room to take their order, she was surprised to hear Fannie and Emily discussing their due dates. This was unusual to her. The Amish women in her former community never discussed their pregnancies, but apparently, it was different here in New Berne.

Abby stood to one side and waited for the end of Fannie and the couple's conversation.

"Emily, does Nate know you're in town?" Fannie asked.

So she's definitely the Emily Nate courted, then.

Abby saw Emily look at her husband before she returned gaze.

"Not yet," Emily said.

Not wanting to eavesdrop any further, Abby hurriedly moved to check on the other diners to see if they needed anything. When she'd confirmed that all was fine, she started across the room to Emily and her husband's table to take their orders. She thought she heard Fannie mention her name and that she was the schoolteacher.

As Abby neared them, Fannie smiled at her. "Emily wants the baked fruit oatmeal special and Abraham would like the griddle corn cakes."

Abby nodded and wrote down their order. It was impossible not to think of Nate as she followed Fannie into the kitchen. "So, Gabriel is Emily's *bruder*?" she asked.

"*Ja*. Gabriel Fisher. You'll meet him tomorrow at Sunday service." Fannie looked thoughtful as she cut a square of the baked oatmeal. "Maybe I should warn Nate that Emily is here before church. Nate's not big on surprises."

Abby didn't reply but she was thinking the same thing. She worked the next hour and a half, taking orders and bringing out food. Soon it was 11 a.m., and the last of the customers—including Abraham and Emily—had left. Abby had been unable to keep her gaze from straying toward Emily and her husband as they'd enjoyed their breakfast. Now that she knew the truth about Nate's past, she worried that he'd be hurt when he saw the woman who'd broken his heart. She understood why Nate had fallen for Emily, as she was a beautiful woman.

"I can tell Nate if you want," she said to Fannie. "We've become friends."

Fannie nodded. "If you could, that'd be *gut*."

Still, Abby felt uncomfortable, imagining what his reaction would be. Why couldn't she warn him that they were here? She and Nate were planning their fake relationship. She could easily check in and talk to him.

By the time she had helped Fannie clean up and set the tables for Monday morning, Abby decided to head to the bakery in town to buy a cake for the midday meal after church tomorrow. On the way back, she'd look for Nate and tell him about Emily and her husband's arrival.

She knew that if it had been she in this situation, Abby would want to know as soon as possible. The last thing she'd want would be to be surprised by an out-of-town ex-love, especially someone who had hurt and wronged her before he'd moved away.

Nate looked around at the work done at the cottage and was pleased with how well it was progressing. He had come as soon as it was light this morning to paint the rooms. So far, he'd finished the bedroom and bathroom and was halfway done with the living room.

He frowned. Nate had expected—hoped—to see Abby here today. Though at first he had dreaded her visits, he now looked forward to seeing her. He had told her they needed to take things slow while establishing a believable basis for their relationship, but he was enjoying becoming her friend.

After church tomorrow, the plan was that he and Abby would spend time together talking. And if she hadn't driven her pony cart to service, he could offer to take her home.

Deciding that he was done for the day, he cleaned up and then left. Determined to avoid Fannie's Restaurant and

Abby's apartment, he drove toward home until the heat of the morning urged him toward Yoder's Ice Cream in town. He turned in its direction, and soon he was in the lot next to the shop, tying up his horse. As he headed toward the front entrance, he recognized Abby's pony cart as she turned onto the bakery lot across the street. He saw her climb down from her vehicle.

"Abby! *Hallo!*" he called. Abby spun and saw him. "Stay there! I'll come to you."

She tied up her horse and then waited for her to join him. She looked especially beautiful today in a dress of solid pink, covered by a white apron and tucked-in cape that made it look as if the apron was full-length. The head coverings worn in her former community had a thick band along the front from just below one ear to the other and a rounded solid white pleated back. In Lancaster County, the band was around the front of the head with strings at each end, made of white organza, a light, almost see-through fabric.

"Hallo," she murmured as she reached his side. Her blond hair was neatly pinned under her *kapp*. "I thought I'd bring a cake tomorrow for the midday meal."

He smiled. "I'm going to get an ice cream sundae. Would you like to join me?"

Although her eyes briefly lit up at the prospect, Abby seemed to hesitate before she gave him a nod. "Let me buy the cake first."

As he met her gaze, he saw wariness in her green eyes. She entered the bakery and he followed her in. She studied the case of bakery items as he stood beside her. "What do you like?" she asked him.

"I like anything." He looked over the baked goods. There were so many that drew his attention. And the scent inside was amazing, tantalizing his hunger, making him want a taste of everything in the showcase. "It all looks *wunderbor*," he admitted. "You choose."

"Chocolate?" she asked with a smile, and he grinned as he gave her a nod. "I'd like that chocolate cake with fudge frosting," she told the girl behind the counter. "And may I have a dozen of those cookies?"

Nate waited quietly next to her as the employee rang up Abby's purchases and handed her the cake and cookie boxes, Abby turned to face him. "Let's go outside and talk," he suggested.

He could feel her tension as she preceded him out of the bakery. "Have a sundae with me while we talk. Yoder's makes the best homemade ice cream. Please?"

"But the cake—" she began.

"We'll put it and the cookies in my buggy. Better there than out in the bright sun." Nate watched her expression war with indecision. "I know it's not lunchtime yet, but ice cream is *gut* no matter what time of day it's eaten." He patiently waited for her answer. Nate was pleased when her lips curved upward.

"Okey," she agreed finally.

They waited for traffic to pass before they crossed the street together with the bakery items. Nate carried the cake while Abby held on to the cookie box. He stored them in the back of his buggy out of the sun's warmth. Then they went inside for their sundaes.

The ice cream parlor was bright and cheery. The tabletops were red Formica with stainless steel trim and the chairs with rounded backs gave the room a homey feel. The menu sign that hung above the counter was extensive, and it took a full minute for Abby to look it over.

"Any idea what you want?" Nate asked her.

"Too many flavors to choose from," she complained.

"But I love chocolate chip mint ice cream with chocolate syrup."

He grinned. "Two chocolate sundaes with chocolate chip mint ice cream." He studied Abby. "Walnuts?"

She shook her head.

"Where would you like to sit?" he asked after he'd paid for their treats and two bottles of water before he handed Abby hers.

Abby seemed to hesitate. "Is there some place to sit outside?"

"*Ja*, there are tables out back." He gestured toward a rear door.

She was quiet as she followed him to a table situated in the shade. "You've been painting," Abby said with a smile now that they were face-to-face across the picnic table.

He beamed at her. "What makes you say that?" he teased.

She smirked at him. "The paint on your face and clothes?"

"Excellent eye, *schule*-teacher," he said with a chuckle. "You have earned passing marks."

They ate in silence for a few minutes.

"You're awfully quiet," he said.

She gave him a small smile, but her usual good humor seemed lacking in her expression. Something must be bothering her. "Can we talk?" she asked.

Nate nodded. He could feel tension thick in the air between them. "Is something wrong?"

"There is something I need to tell you," she rushed on to say. "I'm not sure how you're going to react, and I don't know if I should be the one to tell you at all…but I think you have a right to know."

Nate stilled, his spoon in midair. "What is it?"

"I worked at Fannie's this morning. Linda called in sick." She hesitated. "Someone you know came into the restaurant."

"Who?" he asked quietly.

She seemed unwilling to continue for a moment, but then she blurted out. "Emily and her husband."

Nate felt a rush of air leave his lungs at the startling news.

Chapter Nine

❧

"Are you sure it was Emily Fisher?" Nate asked, stunned by what Abby had told him.

"*Ja*, Fannie greeted her by name, and confirmed she was here to see her brother, Gabriel Fisher." She appeared concerned as she gazed at him. "She's married to Abraham Burkholder." He saw her bite her lip. "And she's... very pretty."

Averting his glance, Nate gave her a nod, his thoughts consumed with how awkward it would be to see them again. He was aware that Abby was staring at him, but he couldn't meet her gaze.

"Nate?" Her soft voice finally drew his attention. "There is something else you need to know."

"*Ja*? What is it?" He couldn't help but be glad she'd warned him.

She hesitated. "Emily...she's with child."

"She's—" Nate felt a painful pang. Emily was pregnant. Why did that bother him so much? He'd thought he was over her—had moved past any feelings for the woman who had rejected him. He wondered what this Abraham looked like. Why she'd chosen this man and not him. And yet even as he wondered, he realized that beyond that initial pang, he didn't truly hurt at the thought of her starting a family with someone else. At most, he felt a little frustration over how her return would stir up gossip about him again. *I am over her*, he realized as he studied Abby's concerned face. Learning she was in town had just startled him.

"Nate, is there anything I can do?" Abby asked, sincerity heavy in her tone.

He thought quickly. It would be awkward to see Emily again accompanied by her husband because she, along with many others, would likely believe he was still pining for her. His fake betrothal with Abby, he realized, would help him convince Emily that he was fine and happy with someone new. "I'm over her, but I'd like to use our fake relationship to fully convince her of that if you're willing," he said. When she appeared as if she was open to the idea, he continued, "We can move up the timeline of our relationship. Instead of casually talking at church tomorrow, I'll pick you up and take you."

"Okey." Abby watched him as if she wondered whether she'd done the right thing in warning him. "I hope I didn't overstep by letting you know about her."

"Nay. I appreciate it," he said as he stood. *"Danki* for telling me." A warmth rose up in him whenever he thought of Abby. He was grateful and pleased that she'd been looking out for him.

"You're *willkomm*," she said softly. "If it were me, I'd want to know." She seemed to freeze. "Nate," she whispered as she stared beyond his shoulder. "They're here."

He stiffened. "Emily and her husband?"

"Ja." She smiled widely at him, playing the part of his sweetheart for their audience, but her green eyes held concern. "They're coming this way."

Nate nodded and was surprised when Abby grabbed a

napkin and leaned across the table to wipe his mouth. He saw a tiny smirk on her face when she sat back.

"Ach, hallo!" she said pleasantly when Emily and her husband came to stand at the far end of their table. "I met you this morning, didn't I?"

"The new teacher," the man nodded. "Nice to see you again."

"Nate," Emily greeted with a smile, ignoring Abby. "How are you?" She looked warmly up at her husband. "I'm sorry, Abe. This is Nate, an old friend of mine. Nate, this is Abraham, my husband."

Nate nodded. *"Gut* to meet you." He reached out to shake hands with the man.

"And you," Abraham said.

Nate shifted his gaze from the man to Emily then back to her husband. "You're adding to your family. Congratulations."

Abraham appeared thrilled. Emily seemed happy about growing her family, but Nate noticed her giving Abby an odd look before returning her attention to him.

"How have you been, Nate?" Emily asked.

Nate looked back to Abby and smiled lovingly. *"Wunderbor."*

Abby grinned at him. "We are both *wunderbor*."

Emily frowned. *"We?"*

"Ja, Nate and I are…ah…close." Abby lowered her voice to a whisper. "We're sweethearts and plan to be much more."

Nate nodded. "It's true. Abby means the world to me." He smiled at Emily. "But don't tell anyone." He laughed to show he wasn't in the least bit concerned if she nattered.

"We should get your ice cream, Em," her husband said, then explained. "Cravings."

"I understand," Abby said with a grin. "Enjoy! We've finished our ice cream, so we'll be on our way."

"Nice meeting you both," Abe said as he led his wife away.

"Enjoy your time with Gabriel!" Abby called out.

"Are you ready?" Nate asked the woman across from him. She'd been wonderfully supportive of him while polite to the couple who had just left.

"Ja." Abby stood as he did and joined him on the other side of the picnic table.

She followed him around the building to the parking lot where he'd parked his vehicle. "Nate? Did I do *oll recht*?"

"You were perfect, Abby." Nate reached for her hand and held on to it, only releasing it once they neared his buggy, where he had stored her cake and cookies earlier.

He heard her sigh. *"Ach, gut."*

He couldn't help but grin at her obvious relief. "I'll be by your apartment at eight to pick you for church," he told her. *"Okey?"*

She nodded "I'll be ready."

Nate realized that he'd come to trust Abby in a short amount of time. More than that, he enjoyed spending time with her—far more than he'd expected when they'd first met. "Service will be at the Bontragers'. You'll like our hosts—Micah and Katie."

Abby looked as if she'd wanted to ask more but then didn't. "Sounds *gut*," she said as they reached his vehicle.

As he opened the door, Nate gestured to the baked goods and said, "I can keep these and bring them tomorrow if you'd like. This way you don't have to worry about them."

She seemed uncertain. "If you're sure..."

"I am." He noticed the traffic had picked up on the road

between the ice cream parlor and the bakery. "Let me walk you across the street," he said.

Her lips curved in a sweet smile. "No need. I know how to avoid cars."

He watched as Abby started toward the road. Suddenly, she halted and came back to him.

"*Danki* for the chocolate sundae."

He felt warmth as he gazed at her. "You're *willkomm*, Abby."

He forced himself to wait when everything inside of him wanted to accompany her as she crossed the street. It wasn't until she was in her vehicle that he got into his buggy and then pulled out onto the shoulder of the road. He was pleased to see her cart follow until she turned onto the parking lot of Fannie's Luncheonette.

Thoughts of Abby stayed with him as he drove home. She turned out to be so much different than he'd first assumed. Kinder. Sweeter. Innocent. Trustworthy. He was glad he'd offered to help her. It turned out that she'd helped him as well. He was going to enjoy his time in their fake relationship until it was over.

Their fake engagement would end after their wedding trip but their friendship? That could continue, couldn't it?

And yet, even if he kept her friendship, Nate didn't want to think about the end of their romance. It wasn't for a while yet.

And the more he envisioned it, the more he wondered if he honestly wanted things with Abby to be over. Or if what he wanted was something much different.

Chapter Ten

Nate pulled his buggy into the row of others parked next to the Bontrager barn. He had come for Abby this morning right on time. She'd been waiting for him near the back door of Fannie's, and they'd exchanged grins as she approached. She wore her royal blue dress, white apron with cape and her new white organza prayer kapp, which she'd purchased at Kings General Store yesterday. Although her money was tight, Abby thought it important for her to fit in with her new community, and her new *kapp* was one way to help. The appreciative look in Nate's gaze when he saw her convinced her that it was money well spent.

While she was at the store, she'd used the pay phone to make a call to New Wilmington to add Nate as her plus-one to her sister's wedding guest list. The store owner who took the call was an old friend who had promised to get word to her family.

Abby looked at the number of vehicles parked beside the barn and marveled that so many families had come for Sunday service. Their congregation back in New Wilmington was much smaller than this one, probably because there were so many church districts in that area. Suddenly, she felt nervous about the time after church when she and Nate would mingle.

"You ready?" he asked.

"Ja," she murmured. *As I'll ever be,* she thought.

He got out and hurried around the vehicle to assist Abby. Then he reached into the back to take out the baked goods.

"I can take those," Abby said when it looked as if Nate planned to carry both boxes.

With a small smile, he handed her the cookies, and she laughed. "You like the chocolate cake, don't you?"

"I do." He led her around the building to the main door. "The *haus* is too small for service, so it will be held in the barn. A few years ago, Micah's barn burned after a lightning strike. This new one was enlarged for gatherings."

As they neared the door, Abby halted. "Are you concerned about seeing Emily again?" she asked softly, to make sure anyone nearby wouldn't overhear.

"Nay," he admitted and smiled at her.

"Gut." Abby was already more than a little nervous attending church service for the first time since Nate had offered to be her sweetheart. Add in Emily and her husband and the woman's possible nattering, and her level of anxiety spiked. But she trusted Nate to make sure she wasn't overwhelmed. "How many families are in your district?"

"About twenty-five," Nate said. "It may seem like a lot of people because of the size of the families." He grinned. "I'm sure Jonas told you how many children will be in school."

"He did. He said I will have twenty-three students." Abby walked next to Nate as she reached the barn door. A group of men were standing in the yard, chatting. Women moved back and forth from the house to the barn. Abby took the cake from Nate and carried the desserts into the kitchen.

"Abby!" Fannie greeted her as she opened the door for her. "I'm glad to see you."

Abby grinned before she stepped inside. "It's *gut* to see you, too." She held up her filled arms. "Where shall I put these?"

Fannie immediately reached for the box of cookies. "We're putting the desserts on the kitchen table."

She followed and added the cake to the table filled with delicious-looking treats. Other women entered the house. A young woman came from a back room.

"Katie, have you met Abby Yost?" Fannie asked, smiling at the pregnant woman.

"Nay." Katie grinned as she approached. *"Hallo,* Abby. I'm Katie Bontrager. I was happy to hear that you'll be our new *schule*-teacher."

Abby liked Katie immediately. She eyed the woman's swollen belly before turning the same attention to Fannie. "Must be something special in the water here," she said with a laugh. The pregnant women chuckled.

The back door opened, and a man stuck his head in. "Church will be starting soon."

"Danki, Micah." Katie smiled at him with love. "We'll be right out."

Abby felt her heart melt at the affection between Katie and her husband. Their type of marriage was what she'd always longed for.

"Do you need help with our *kinner*?" Micah asked.

"Nay, I'll manage," his wife assured him. "James is a toddler and can be a handful," she told Abby after her husband left.

"I'd be happy to help with him," Abby found herself offering. "I love children. If you want, I can hold James during service."

Katie beamed at her. *"Wunderbor.* That would be a big

help. *Danki.* I'll get the little ones from their room. Our eldest *soohn*, Jacob, has been watching them for me."

The barn had been set up for service. Benches had been set in rows for the men and in another area the women with children. A wooden pulpit had been placed up front. Seated next to Katie with the woman's son James on her lap, Abby studied her surroundings with awe.

"This barn is perfect for church," she commented to Katie beside her.

The service started as folks stood and began the opening hymn, singing in high German. Afterward, Jonas Miller took to the pulpit, rising from the group of church elders who were seated in the front row of the men's section. She listened carefully as he did a reading and then talked about it. His sermon was inspiring and called to her. She silently praised *Gott* for bringing her here to New Berne to start life over with people who were genuinely kind and giving.

During the service, James struggled a bit on her lap a time or two but Abby was able to calm him with soft words and a pat on the back. He was about two or three years old, Abby surmised. She imagined he could be a handful, but she knew that Katie had help in his older siblings and her husband, Micah.

While she was listening to the sermons, she couldn't help but glance Nate's way from time to time. To her surprise and delight, he was watching her every time she did. She felt a rush of warmth for the man who cared enough to support her at her sister's wedding. And now she was able to help him as well to deal with the past and the present.

She felt someone's eyes on her a few times, and she had a feeling that it was Emily who was curious about her. Abby refused to look back and give the woman any ability to read her thoughts or expression. She caught Nate's gaze again and gave him a small smile. He didn't return it but continued to gaze at her as if fascinated.

The service eventually ended. The women and children headed toward the house while the men moved the church benches outside where the communal meal would be served. Carrying James, Abby followed Katie into the house. The kitchen bustled with some women removing food from the refrigerator to set out on the countertops while others grabbed dishes to take out to the food tables.

Katie reached for her youngest, and Abby relinquished little James into his mother's arms. "I'm going to feed him now. He's due for a nap, but he'll sleep longer if he's got a full belly." She put him in his high chair out of the way of the women coming and going.

"What can I do to help?" Abby asked.

"You've already been a big help today." Katie opened the pantry and took out a box of cereal. She sprinkled some on the tray of James's high chair.

"You look tired." Abby eyed her with sympathy. "Why don't you sit for a bit? I can feed James."

Katie gazed at her with gratitude. "*Danki.* I can see you'll be a *wunderbor* teacher. It's clear you love children."

Abby inclined her head. "I do." She watched James eat the cereal with his little hands. "Does he drink milk?"

"*Ja.*" Her new friend gestured to a wall cabinet. "You'll find his sippy cup up there."

After getting the boy's cup, Abby filled it partially with milk. She set it on the tray, prepared in case James decided to throw or drop it. She felt a sense of satisfaction when the toddler reached for the cup and drank deeply before putting it down again. It didn't take long for him to finish his cereal. "Will he eat more?"

"*Ja*, just a little." Katie rubbed her protruding belly as

if soothing an ache there. "Perfect," she said after Abby added another small mound of cereal.

Abby wondered if she should be outside where Nate was bound to be waiting for her. But Emily had entered the house and wasn't anywhere near him to make him uncomfortable, so Abby figured it would be all right to help Katie for a little longer.

A few minutes later Katie carried James off to bed and Abby went outside to join Nate. She found him under a shade tree talking with a group of men. When he caught her eye, he excused himself and headed her way.

"I'm sorry to have kept you waiting," she said. "I was helping Katie with her *kinner*. With five children in the *haus* and one on the way, she's exhausted."

"That's fine." Nate seemed pleased to see her. "Neither Abraham nor Emily has approached to talk with me."

Abby was relieved. "Emily is in the *haus*." She saw that the tables and benches had been set up for the meal. "Are we allowed to sit together or do the men eat first and then the women with children?"

Nate smiled. "We can eat together. Our community allows us to do what we want, especially when dining outside."

"Shall we sit at a table, then?" she asked.

"Ja." His brown eyes studied her as if he'd noticed something different about her.

"What? Do I have something on my face?" She lifted a hand to touch her cheek, which was hot from his intense inspection.

"Nay." He grinned. "I saw you holding James during service."

She frowned. *"Okey.* Did I do something wrong?"

Nate shook his head as he led her to a table. "You're a

natural with children. James is young and usually has trouble sitting still but you managed to keep him calm. I think he even fell asleep for a while. No wonder you want to be a teacher. You like being around little ones."

Abby blushed. "I love *kinner*. I enjoy spending time with them."

He didn't say anything, and she got the sense he was thinking hard about something. What, she had no idea.

She stood up from the table. "What would you like to eat? I'll get our plates."

"You don't have to bring me food, Abby," he said, meeting her gaze. "I'll go with you."

There was a line at the food tables. Nate waited behind Abby for their turn at the dishes spread out before them. "Your *schweschter*'s wedding is coming up soon," he said. "I know you're not looking forward to it, but I'll be with you."

"I know." Abby felt suddenly emotional. "I'm so grateful for you...and your help, Nate." She'd begun to trust him like no other man since Peter. Her heart warmed as she gazed at him before she glanced away.

"We're helping each other," he said softly. "You and I are friends, Abby, aren't we?"

She nodded, wondering why she felt disappointed by the idea of being nothing more than "friends."

They filled up their plates and returned to the table with food and drinks. Nate settled in his seat next to her.

"I can buy us bus tickets for the drive to New Wilmington for the wedding," he told her.

She shook her head. "That doesn't seem right, Nate."

"Why not? We're together—you and me." His genuine smile filled her heart with joy.

"*Ja*, but it's my *schweschter*'s wedding." And the dread of attending returned to haunt her.

Nate took her mind off the worry as he began to tell her about the progress he'd made on the cottage yesterday. Abby asked questions, and he answered with patience. She was so engaged in their conversation that it took her a few minutes to realize that a couple had sat down across from them.

"Abraham," she greeted. With a smile in Nate's direction, she covered his hand on the table. "Emily, are you enjoying your visit with your *bruder*?"

Emily nodded. "*Ja*, it's been great to see him again. It's been too long since I visited. Lucy is a fine wife, and he is happy with her. I enjoy talking with my sister-in-law about being a mother."

Abby smiled. "I'm sure your *bruder* and Lucy are glad you've come." She studied the blond woman in front of her and wondered exactly what Nate had seen in her. She was beautiful, Abby gave her that, but she didn't think Nate would go for looks alone. "And it is always a blessing when a couple finds happiness together. I look forward to happily spending the rest of my life with Nate."

"I feel the same." A hint of amusement twinkled in Nate's light brown eyes. "So, Abraham, what do you do for a living?"

"I'm a farmer," the man said, and Abby felt Nate tense up beside her. She remembered him telling her that Emily's excuse for not marrying him was that she didn't want to be a farmer's wife.

"What do you farm?" Abby asked, curious, as she placed a hand gently on Nate's back, hoping to soothe him.

"Apples." The man smiled at his wife. "We own a large

apple orchard in Ohio. May eventually put in other fruit trees as well."

"That's *wunderbor*. It must be nearly harvesting time for you."

"It is," Emily said.

Abby nodded. "We are looking to buy a farm."

"We?" Emily narrowed her gaze as she looked Abby up and down.

"*Ja*, we as in Abby and me," Nate said with a smile.

Abby managed to conceal her amusement. "This week we plan to look at properties with a *haus*."

Emily was conspicuously quiet, but her husband appeared pleased for them. "That's *wunderbor* news, Nate," Abraham said.

Nate gazed at Abby with what could only be seen as a loving glance. It made Abby feel warm and pleased but then she recalled it was only an act, one that would end after her sister's wedding.

Emily appeared disturbed as she studied her and Nate together.

"When is your little one due?" Abby dared to ask.

"In two months." Emily's expression softened. "We're looking forward to it."

"Abby and I plan to have children," Nate said with a smile full of real joy. She could see that he truly wanted to be a father, and she knew he'd be a *gut* one, once he found the right woman. It just made her sad to think that it wouldn't be her.

Despite her past heartbreak at the hands of her sister and Peter, she found herself more drawn to Nate with each passing day. She liked talking to him. Not only did he listen to her problems with genuine concern, but he'd also offered to help her. She cared for him so much already, and she knew that her feelings would only grow as long as they kept up the act.

But, she reminded herself, if her feelings got hurt in the end, she'd have no one to blame but herself. This wasn't like the situation with Peter. Nate had been nothing but honest with her. She'd known from the start that he wasn't offering her a real relationship. This arrangement with Nate was only temporary, and soon it would be over.

Chapter Eleven

"Where are we going first?" Abby asked as Nate drove down the road. He had arranged to view a few properties this morning.

"There's a property for sale not far from here," he told her. "I figured we'd start looking there."

Before they'd parted on Sunday after the midday meal, she reminded him about searching for property for his dairy farm. Nate had said he had things he needed to do on Monday and they could start the property search today, Tuesday morning.

"Abraham and Emily leave tomorrow?" she commented, seeking confirmation.

"I heard they left today," Nate said. "Abraham was eager to get home to ready his apple orchards for the upcoming harvest."

"Ach." She bit her lip. "You don't have to take me with you," she said. "I know I said all those things to your Emily and her husband, but it's not my place to go."

"I want you to come with me, Abby. Looking at property together is a *gut* idea," he said, sounding sincere. "I value your opinion, and it's nice to have your company." He wore a smile as he captured and held her gaze.

She released a long breath. *"Okey."* Pleased by his

words, Abby couldn't help enjoying the make-believe of pretending that she and Nate really were planning their future together.

After a short ride, Nate pointed. "There. On the left. Our first stop." He pulled onto the driveway. The house wasn't far from the road but away enough to have a bit of privacy.

"There's no For Sale sign. How did you learn about this?" Abby climbed down from his buggy before he could help her.

"Jonas gave me the information. He is a *gut* source, who knows what's going on in our community." Nate flashed her a grin. "I've worked for him for over three years now. He is a *wunderbor* boss and a friend. I trust him like no other." She wondered what it would be like to have Nate's full trust. She'd thought him surly and rude at first, but as she'd learned more about him, she realized there was so much more to him than that. He was someone worthy of love and commitment.

"Is anyone living here?" she asked.

Nate shook his head. "Jonas said the couple who owns this property recently moved out. They were eager to move closer to their oldest *soohn*."

He tied up his horse. "Let's check out the fields first," he said. "I can always fix the *haus* if it needs work, but I need acreage for my cows to graze when they're not yet ready for the milking barn."

Abby followed him to a fenced-in pasture behind the house. The pasture seemed to go on as far as her eyes could see. "It's lovely here," she murmured, taken by the beauty of the land. "Is there a place to put milking and calving barns?" Nate had told her about his plans, and she had learned from him all of the things a dairy farm required.

"Maybe there," he said, gesturing toward an open spot

behind the house to the right. "It may be best if I build a large enough barn that it can be used as both. Two areas separate from each other."

She smiled. "*Ja*, that would be a *wunderbor* place for it." She could see how such a huge outbuilding would work— the new dairy and calving barn with fencing or walls between the two sections. And the farmhouse? She had no idea what it looked like inside but she envisioned a nice place to live with an eat-in kitchen, large gathering room, and plenty of bedrooms for a big family.

Nate was quiet a moment before he turned back to the residence on the property. "I can envision a herd of my dairy cows grazing in the fields here." He smiled at her. "Shall we look inside the *haus*?"

"Do you have a key?" Abby fell into step beside him and grinned when he held it up.

When they reached the back door, he unlocked it and they stepped inside.

"Nice!" she exclaimed as they entered the house. "What is this? A mudroom?" It was a small room with a vinyl floor and a washing machine.

"*Ja*," Nate said with a hum. "Let's check out the kitchen and other rooms."

She followed him through the mudroom into the kitchen area. The cabinets were oak and in wonderful condition. The countertops appeared new. The stove was woodburning, and the sink had a window above it like the one Nate had put into the teacher's cottage. "Doesn't look like any work needs to be done. Except maybe a gas range for cooking." She faced him. "You could change the woodburning stove into a heater for the *haus*."

He locked gazes with her and smiled. "Shall we check out the rest of the rooms?"

Abby bobbed her head. "*Ja*, please. So far everything is more than I ever expected."

There was a half bathroom downstairs—only a toilet and sink. The living area was spacious, and Abby could easily see a family with friends enjoying an afternoon there. Next, she trailed behind Nate up the stairs to the second floor. There were four bedrooms—two of a decent size and two that were much smaller but would certainly do for young children. The walls had a fresh coat of paint. The wooden floors looked clean and shiny. She loved everything about the house so much that she doubted that the other properties they were planning to see could possibly be better than this one. The upstairs bathroom had a shower with a tub. Everything appeared spick-and-span, and Abby fell a little more in love with every detail as she studied her surroundings.

Without a word, Nate started down the stairs, and Abby fell into step behind him. They left the house, locking the door behind them. Then he stopped and turned to her. "What do you think?"

Abby smiled. "I like it. A lot."

"Hmm" was all he said. Then, "Let's check out the next property."

Nate was thinking hard as they headed toward the second property, located a few miles farther from town. He liked the farm they'd left. He could tell how much Abby liked it, too. That he could see her living there with him shook him. This relationship wasn't real and to dream about more would be a painful mistake. He shouldn't forget that.

As he pulled onto the driveway at the second place, he was already disappointed in the condition of the house. It needed a lot of work. There was siding missing along the front of the house. The porch looked rickety and unsafe.

Nate could only imagine what the interior was like. He had no real desire to go inside to find out. Still, he drove his buggy up close to it and climbed down to survey the surrounding farmland. The land looked overgrazed. There was a barn but it was too dilapidated to use. He stopped near the fence and knew the exact second when Abby joined him.

"Nate, I know this isn't really my business," she said, "but you asked for my opinion. Even if it's cheaper than the other one, this place needs too much work."

He didn't respond at first. Finally, he met her gaze. "I agree." He hid a smile as he heard her quiet sigh of relief. "I don't think I need to look elsewhere, do you?"

"It's going to be your home," she said softly, averting her eyes to look down at her sneakers.

"*Ja*, it is," he agreed. "Let's go back. I need to talk with Jonas to see if the seller on the first property is willing to take slightly less than the asking price. I'll take you back to your apartment first."

Nate dropped Abby off before going to see Jonas. He felt her disappointment as they parted and he left. As he steered his horse toward Miller's Dairy Farm, he found that he missed her company. He was getting too used to spending most of his time with her. It worked to convince everyone that they were courting, but what would he do when they let that pretense go? With the changes in Clara's marriage schedule, her sister's wedding was now next week. Once they returned from New Wilmington, there would be no reason to keep up the ruse with Abby. He didn't like the thought of going back to how things had been before. He hadn't realized how lonely he'd been before Abby had come into his life.

A painful pang hit him in his chest. He forced thoughts of Abby away. Nate knew he had to concentrate on purchasing his farm. That was where his future lay—not with a woman who was only pretending to be in love with him.

Jonas came out of the milking barn as Nate drove onto the property. The man smiled and approached as Nate climbed down from his vehicle and met him halfway.

"Well?" the preacher said. "What did you think of the places you saw?"

"We like the Emmett Beiler farm," Nate said.

"We?" Jonas asked with a twinkle in his eyes.

"Abby came with me," he admitted, feeling his face flush with heat. "Because... Because I value her opinion."

"She's a lovely young woman," Jonas teased. "You and she make a *gut* couple."

Nate started to open his mouth to object, then quickly closed it. Because Jonas was right. He and Abby made a good couple. The fact that Jonas felt that way let him know that everyone truly believed he and Abby were sweethearts. And that was what they wanted. For everyone to think they were together. For now, anyway.

Nate and Jonas discussed what he should offer for the property. If the sellers weren't willing to take less, he could afford to buy it anyway. It would be tight for him at first but he'd manage. Still, it was worth a try to see if it could get a lower price. Jonas seemed to think that Emmett Beiler would accept the lower offer. Emmett was eager to sell but he also wanted someone who would care for his property and beloved home that he had left behind.

"I'll reach out to Emmett with your offer," Jonas promised. "As soon as I know something, I'll contact you, whether he accepts your offer or not."

"*Danki* for your help," Nate said, relieved to have such a fine friend to rely on.

Nate left Miller's Dairy Farm, feeling better after talking with Jonas, who would soon be his former employer. He would always be grateful to the man for hiring him and teaching him so much about dairy farming.

His first thought as he left was to visit Abby and ask if she'd like to take a ride. A lot had been done to the cottage since the last time she was there. In fact, it was nearly finished. He'd said as much to Jonas who promised to make sure the furniture was ordered and delivered in a week or less so Abby could move into her new home well before school started. He'd gotten a good start on the schoolhouse as well. The outside brick had been repaired and repainted. He still had Abby's bookcases to build and the interior to whitewash but that wouldn't take long since Abby had scrubbed the walls to make painting them easier.

It wasn't long before he pulled onto the paved lot behind Fannie's. Nate entered through the back door like he usually did. Fannie came out of the kitchen with a plate in each hand.

"Nate," she said. "Coming in for lunch?"

He shook his head, although he was hungry and could eat. "I'm here to see Abby. Is she upstairs?"

"*Ja.* Go on up," Fannie told him. "She went up when she got back, and I haven't seen her since."

"I'll take those," Linda insisted, reaching for the platters in Fannie's hands.

Fannie sighed. "I can handle a few dishes."

"I'm sure you can but if you don't want your doctor to tell you not to work at all, then I suggest you take it easier." Linda gazed at her employer and friend with concern. "Go and put your feet up. Have you had a lunch yet?"

"No, she hasn't," Linda's sister, Esther, said. Esther worked part-time at Fannie's. "She's been on her feet all morning, cooking."

"I'll make you something special," Linda promised. "Let me serve these first."

Nate was relieved to see the two sisters pitching in and forcing Fannie to rest. He didn't want to have to tell Jonas that his pregnant daughter was working too hard, but he would have if she had no help.

He opened the bottom door. "Abby! It's Nate," he called up the staircase.

Abby appeared at the top of the steps. "Nate! You came back."

"*Ja.* I wanted to let you know what Jonas said. And to ask if you'd like to go for a ride with me." He watched as she started down the steps toward him. He felt a flutter in his stomach as he realized just how much he was drawn to her. She looked beautiful in a spring green dress that made her green eyes look brighter. "Have you eaten?"

She shook her head. "Not yet. I haven't been hungry."

"Come with me. I'll show you something and make sure you eat." He moved back through the door opening and into the hallway as she reached the bottom landing. "So, you'll go with me?"

With a smile, she bobbed her head. "You have me curious now."

Nate grinned at her. *"Gut."* He preceded her to the back door and opened it, holding it wide for her to leave the building first. "Do you like hot dogs?"

"I do," she said as he helped her into his buggy.

He climbed onto the driver's seat and faced her. "There's this little stand that sells the best frankfurters one can order with any toppings you'd like."

Abby regarded him with delight. "It sounds *wunderbor!*"

They stopped for lunch first. He was pleased when she

ordered the same thing as him—a dog all the way, which included a special chili meat sauce, chopped onions and mustard underneath. When he offered to buy her a side of French fries instead of sharing his, she declined, telling him that if he was fine with it, she'd eat only one or two of his. They each had a root beer. While they enjoyed lunch, Nate brought her up to date on his conversation with Jonas and the offer for the property that the preacher was going to make on his behalf.

"I'm still hoping to pay a little less than the asking price." Nate smiled. "Jonas said that Emmett Beiler, the man who owns it, is more anxious to have someone live there who will care about the property and *haus*. And you know I do." He paused and then added, "We both do. It's just what I need for my dairy farm."

Abby seemed genuinely pleased for him. "I'm happy for you, Nate. I knew as soon as I saw the farm and residence that it would be perfect for you."

Nate nodded. He was probably telling her more than he should, but he valued her opinion. Plus, she was so easy to talk to. It felt so natural to be with her—almost as if their courtship was real and they really were planning a future together. But her heart was still hurting from the man who'd chosen her sister over her. He knew what a blow that had given her. He remembered how he'd felt when Emily had rejected his proposal. Even though he no longer had any feelings for Emily, he hadn't forgotten what she'd put him through, and he had no desire to feel that kind of pain again.

When he saw that Abby was done eating, he stood and collected their garbage, tossing it in the trash pail. He smiled gently as he returned to her. "Ready to finish our ride?"

"You have me wondering where you're planning on taking me," she said with a small smile.

He laughed. "You'll have to wait and see."

Nate drove a roundabout way to the teacher's cottage to keep her from guessing their destination. He drove up the lane to the end and flashed her a grin when she looked surprised that he had brought her here.

"I thought you'd like to see the progress I've made since the last time you were here," he told her as he climbed out and then helped her. He led Abby around the house to the door on the front porch. Wanting to surprise her, he'd doubled down on his workload with hours well into the night. He'd managed to garner help from Fannie in keeping Abby away for a couple of days and now he wanted to see her reaction.

"Close your eyes," he urged. Once she obeyed, he unlocked the door and led her inside. "Go ahead and open them."

Nate studied her face as she took in her surroundings. With the help of Jed and another friend who'd assisted him with the floors and kitchen cabinets installation, nearly everything was done, and he was quite pleased with how the completed work looked.

She blinked with a gaping mouth. "How did you get all this done?"

"Jed and Michael, another friend, helped," he told her, pleased by her reaction.

"It seems finished," she said with amazement. "*Is* it finished?"

"Just about. By the time we head to New Wilmington next week, you'll have the furniture Jonas and Fannie picked out and ordered, and you'll be able to move in." Nate became worried when he saw tears fill her green eyes. "Abby?"

With a chuckle, she reached up to wipe them away. "These are happy tears, Nate."

Nate closed his eyes briefly. *Praise the Lord.*

He hadn't realized just how much he needed her to like it until now.

Chapter Twelve

Abby had been amazed when two days after he'd showed her the finished cottage, it appeared ready to move in. She stood in the middle of the bedroom, fighting tears. She loved the furniture that the church community had provided for her...the double bed with wooden head and foot boards, with a beautiful blue quilt covering the mattress, and pillows. The dresser was of the same oak with six drawers, more than enough for a schoolteacher's needs. As she ran her hand over the smooth finish, she felt Nate's quiet presence behind her, watching her, waiting for her reaction.

"What do you think?" he asked in a deep, rumbling voice.

With watery eyes, she turned to the man who had made this all possible. She sniffed once before answering. "It's... perfect."

A bright light lit up his gorgeous brown gaze. "I'm glad you like it."

Her tears spilled down her cheeks. "I'm amazed how quickly everything came together."

Nate gazed at her, looking worried. "Happy tears?"

She beamed. "*Ja*, tears of joy."

He grinned. *"Gut."*

"I appreciate this all," she said as she swept her hand around the room. "And everyone in the community. I've never felt this appreciated in my entire life." She was startled but pleased when Nate reached for her hand and squeezed it briefly before letting go.

"It's been a pleasure to do this for you," he said. "We're all grateful you accepted the teaching position and moved here."

She studied Nate with warmth in her chest. "I'm the one who's grateful, Nate." He was wonderful and she thanked *Gott* for bringing him into her life. Nate had built her the ideal house with everything she'd ever wanted inside. And the kind, honorable man was also helping her by offering to accompany her to Clara's wedding.

"I never thought you could work this hard," she teased.

"I felt motivated." He chuckled. "Would you like to move in today?" he asked, his brown eyes twinkling.

Abby felt her excitement build, threatening to make her laugh and cry as she felt a deep welling of emotions. "I can do that?"

"*Ja.* We can go to your apartment now and get all your things." Nate smiled. "Would you like that?"

She bobbed her head. "I would."

He looked amused but pleased. "Let's go. It's early and you can settle in your home before I take you to lunch."

She laughed. "You're going to feed me again?"

"We need to eat, don't we?" He led her through the cottage without rushing her as she took in once again the living room and kitchen with all new furniture in both rooms.

"Where are you going to take me?" she said coyly, overjoyed with how well her day was going.

"Have you ever had Chinese food?" He opened the back door and waited for her to exit the house before him.

"*Nay,* I can't say I ever have." She stopped and faced him. "Have you?"

He chuckled. "*Nay,* but I thought it would be something different to try."

"I'm willing," she assured him.

This playful side of Nate was entirely different from the man she'd first met who had been angry and distant in their interactions. It was hard to equate this sweet, thoughtful person with that former Nate.

Two hours later, after they'd ordered and waited for their food, she and Nate were back at the cottage. She had packed up her meager belongings and moved in. They were now seated at the kitchen table across from each other, four cartons of Chinese food on the table between them. Abby had been surprised to find that not only had Fannie and Jonas made sure she had nice furniture but they had also loaded her kitchen cabinets with dishes and cups, and they'd placed silverware and dish towels in the drawers. A pantry closet had a nice array of basic foods as well as the essentials for baking. Dairy products including milk, butter and eggs were in the refrigerator. She'd never felt this cherished before, which made her sad that her own family had never made her feel loved. But that was her past. This was her future—and it looked bright.

"How's your chicken and broccoli?" Nate asked before he raised a forkful of beef and green beans to his mouth.

"It's delicious. Want to try some?" She pushed the pint of the chicken dish to him across the table. She'd chosen white rice while Nate had decided on fried rice. "White rice?"

Nate shook his head. "I'll eat the chicken if you'll taste my beef dish."

They chatted as they enjoyed their meal. Abby thought it was good but she preferred the hot dogs they'd eaten at the small outdoor stand. When they were done, she put the leftovers in the refrigerator and then returned to the table to talk about their trip next week.

"The wedding will be on Tuesday," Abby said. "We'll

need to leave on Monday and find somewhere to stay for the night. The ceremony starts early, so we'll need to stay somewhere close by." She met Nate's gaze and saw him nod. "There's a nice bed-and-breakfast in New Wilmington near my parents' place. We can stay one or two nights there, depending on when we want to go home."

"How do you know about this place?" he asked.

"I know the owners," she told him. She was grateful that he didn't ask why she didn't plan to stay with her family. The truth was, she didn't feel she had a place there. Maybe she'd never had one, not really.

Feeling teary again, she blinked and stood, turning her back to Nate before he could see. Unlike her family, he'd worry if he realized she was crying.

Abby heard the light scrape of his chair across wood. She stared out through the window over the sink, praying for the Lord to help her, to grant her peace.

"Abby?" he murmured, and she could feel him step up behind her. His hands settled on her shoulders and turned her toward him. "What's wrong?"

She shook her head. "I'm *oll recht*," she said.

His hands slid down her arms to catch her hands. "You're not, but you will be."

Meeting his gaze, Abby managed a wobbly smile. "My family..."

"I understand," he said, and although she didn't explain, his expression, filled with compassion and warmth, told her that he truly did understand.

Nate was thoughtful as he watched Abby. He couldn't imagine why her family treated her the way they did. Not that he doubted her account—especially after his encounter with Clara. For whatever reason, her family failed to appreciate the amazing woman that she was. He could only feel sorry for them for not realizing what they'd had. He watched as she went to the table and picked up their empty plates then placed them in the sink.

"Let me help you with the dishes," he said as she pulled a plastic dish rack with drain mat from the cabinet under the sink.

Abby shook her head. "You bought the food. The least I can do is wash dishes."

"If you want to do them now, please let me dry them." Nate opened a drawer and pulled out a dish towel.

He heard her sigh. *"Okey,"* she agreed.

It took them no time at all to finish. After the dishes were put away, Nate leaned back against the counter. "So, we'll leave Monday morning to New Wilmington," he said, "and we'll check into the bed-and-breakfast once we get there."

"Ja," Abby said "I called and made reservations with the owners. I can always change or cancel them."

Nate smiled his thanks when she handed him a chocolate cookie. "You'll be coming with me to the Fishers for Visiting Day on Sunday, won't you?"

She took a sip of her iced tea before answering. "If I'm invited."

"You're most definitely invited. I spoke with Lucy the other day and she wanted to make sure we'll both be there." He bit into his cookie and hummed with pleasure at the delicious burst of chocolate flavor. "I'll stop by and pick you up…if you don't mind going with me."

"Why would I mind? After all, we're fake sweethearts." The bright smile on her face made him catch his breath. "I'd love to go with you." She suddenly looked worried. "What shall I bring?"

"Nothing. I have us covered. I picked up two dozen

brownies yesterday from the bakery we visited last week." He was happy to see her relax.

She reached into the box for a peanut butter cookie, then took a bite. "What time should we leave on Sunday?"

"I'll come for you at eight thirty. *Oll recht*?"

"Sounds *gut* to me." Once they'd finished with their cookies and tea, Abby stood. "I appreciate everything you've done for me, Nate."

"What have I done?" he teased. "I don't recall doing anything but enjoy your company."

He felt warm inside when he saw her blush with pleasure.

"Let me show you a few things in the *haus*," Nate said, "to make sure you feel comfortable and safe."

"Danki," she murmured.

Abby seemed emotional as he took her through every room and showed her how to ensure her windows were locked. Then he instructed her on the use of the washing machine. "I'll hang a clothesline for you," Nate said. "Michael and Jed promised to build you a small barn for your horse and pony cart while we're away."

Although it was still light outside, because of the summer hours, Nate knew that he should leave so Abby could get settled in her new home.

"I have one more thing to give you," he said as he headed out the back door to his buggy. She followed behind him.

"What is it?" she asked, sounding intrigued.

He pulled out a box that he'd stored under the back seat earlier and handed it to her. "It's a cell phone. We aren't allowed house phones, but we can have mobile phones. Call if you need anything. I already programmed my phone number in it. Don't hesitate to reach out to me if you have a problem or just need to talk about one thing or the other."

"Where did you get this?" she asked. "Did you pay for it?"

"Our church elders bought it for you," he assured her. "They wanted to ensure you have a way to reach out in case of an emergency with the children at school. And they will take care of the monthly bill for you. The phone is charged, and there is a fully charged power pack with it to recharge the phone when needed. You can recharge the pack and the phone, if you want, at Fannie's Luncheonette or Kings General Store." He smiled. "I can show you how to use it."

She bobbed her head. "*Danki*. That would be *wunderbor*. I don't know anything about cell phones." She gave him a crooked smile. "I'll feel better knowing that I can reach you if needed." Then she appeared embarrassed, and he was delighted by the bright red that stained her cheeks.

"I'll be by tomorrow to check on you, and we can finish making plans for Monday." Nate studied her lovely features. "Anything else you need to know?"

"*Nay*, I have everything I need." Clutching the box to her, she waited while he climbed into his vehicle. She waved at him as he left, and he wished he had an excuse to stay longer. But they would be together for Visiting Day, then the trip to New Berne, the wedding and then the bus ride home.

Spending time with Abby Yost made his head spin, and thoughts of her remained, making him long to return to her. Home once again, he received a phone call.

"Emmett Beiler has accepted your offer for the property," Jonas said as soon as Nate answered. "He knows of your construction work and feels that you'll take *gut* care of his *haus* and land."

Excited, Nate found that his first thought after he hung up with Jonas was to call Abby. But he would wait until he saw her next. He wanted to see her reaction to his news.

An hour later, he couldn't hold it in and dialed Abby's cell number.

"Hallo?" She sounded timid, as if she was overwhelmed by her new phone.

"Abby, it's Nate. I wanted to tell you that my offer for the farm was accepted," he said.

"That's *wunderbor*, Nate!" Abby exclaimed. "I'm so happy for you." Her reaction ramped up his excitement. "We should celebrate."

He chuckled. "We will. As soon as I'm settled on the property."

When he hung up, Nate sat in a kitchen chair with a huge grin on his face. His dream of a dairy farm was within his grasp, and soon he and Abby would spend days together. He looked forward to the trip with Abby.

He sent *Gott* a silent prayer, asking that everything go according to plan at the wedding for Abby's sake. He knew it wouldn't be an easy thing for her to watch, and he worried about how she might respond. While watching her sister wed her former betrothed, would Abby withdraw from him? From the idea of having a relationship with anyone? It would be understandable if that happened. Surely the wisest thing for him to do would be to give her the space she needed to deal with her feelings. It wouldn't be right to ask her for a real relationship when she already had so much weighing on her heart.

And his heart was still fragile as well. Too fragile to risk another rejection.

This good news about the property should invigorate him to focus on his goals of starting a farm, not a new romance he wasn't sure either he or Abby were ready for. Yet even as he cautioned himself, he knew how much he liked having Abby around as a friend. And he realized with dread how much he wanted that friendship to grow into something more.

Chapter Thirteen

❧

Nate studied the town through the bus window as he and Abby drove through Clearfield. He couldn't see much, but it appeared to be a nice place.

"We're close to the halfway point to New Wilmington." She sat in the aisle seat next to Nate but leaned closer to him for a better view of the scenery they passed. He detected the scent of her soap or shampoo that smelled like vanilla and felt the brush of her hair across his arm as she strived to get a better look at the stop and surrounding area.

"We could stay here on the way back if you want," he suggested.

"We could, but it's probably not a *gut* idea." She turned her head to look at him, and with a gasp she straightened, realizing she had invaded his space. "I'm sorry."

"What for?" Nate already knew but he wanted to see her reaction.

She blushed. "I leaned over you."

He shrugged "So?"

Abby blinked several times until she realized that he was teasing her. "You!"

"It's fine. We're in a relationship after all, *ja*?"

"True." She grinned at him, and he was enchanted with her pretty, green eyes, her adorably pert nose and her wide smile of amusement. She glanced at her watch as the bus continued its way toward New Wilmington. "Are you hungry?"

She'd made them both sandwiches and brought cookies. He'd brought cans of sweet cold tea. Nate locked eyes with her. "A little," he admitted.

Abby unzipped her tote and reached in for their lunch. She handed him a sandwich, and he gave her the sweet tea.

"How much time until we get there?" Nate took a bite from his lunch and enjoyed the delicious taste of ham and Swiss cheese on rye bread.

She popped the top on her iced tea can. "Another two hours, at least."

He watched her take a sip from her drink before setting it in the cup holder by her seat. Then she took a bite of her sandwich and grinned. "I love ham and cheese. I enjoy it grilled even more, but this works."

"It does," he said. They ate silently for a time, aware of the *Englishers* on the bus who couldn't seem to stop staring at them. He did his best to ignore them, and eventually he felt their interest wane.

When they were done eating their sandwiches, Abby handed him the box of cookies but didn't take any for herself. "I think I'll close my eyes and rest for a while."

Nate set the box in the pouch on the back of the seat in front of him. "Let's trade places. I need to sit on the outside where I can protect you while you sleep."

She regarded him with surprise. "I'll be fine—"

"Abby," he said firmly. "Please."

With a sleepy nod, she got up the same time as he did and they switched seats. He wasn't sure why she'd insisted on taking the aisle seat in the first place. The few times she wanted to see something outside, she'd had to lean over, making him overly conscious of every little thing about her.

"Rest," he told her as she got comfortable in the seat. She lay back and closed her eyes. He smiled when her breath eventually evened out as she slept.

They had both put their larger pieces of luggage under the bus before they'd gotten on that morning, keeping smaller ones with them. Nate reached under the seat and pulled out his zippered bag to retrieve a blanket. He unfolded it and carefully covered Abby. The air-conditioning was cool and he worried about her comfort. When she snuggled beneath it, he smiled and then watched over her as she slept, enjoying every moment of the trip with her. He liked just being with her. Even if their relationship never went beyond friendship, he was happy to be her friend.

Abby started to wake up slowly, relaxed and comfy where she was snuggled under a blanket, until she realized she wasn't in bed. She'd fallen asleep sitting up. The sound of an engine with a sensation of vibration below her seat startled her into full wakefulness. She gasped and sat up, confused for a second before she remembered she was on a bus. Her gaze settled on the man in the seat beside her. *Nate.* She was on a bus with Nate and they were headed to New Wilmington for Clara's wedding to Peter, the man she'd loved who had jilted her for her sister.

I don't love Peter anymore. She sighed and closed her eyes. *Nay*, she cared for Nate now. More than she ever cared for anyone in her life. And that scared her. No one she'd loved had ever truly loved her back before.

"Are you *oll recht*?" Nate asked.

Abby locked gazes with him, trying to hide her feelings. She nodded. "I'm fine. I was just disoriented for a moment."

She shifted, pulling the quilt higher over her shoulders. "You gave me this," she said with a small smile. *"Danki."*

He shifted to face her more fully. "I was afraid you'd get cold."

"Aren't *you* cold?" She loved that he'd thought of her, but she hadn't wanted him to sacrifice his own comfort for her.

Nate shook his head. "I'm warm enough." He looked past her through the window. "It won't be long now."

"Do you know how close we are?" Nerves began to attack her. It wasn't seeing Peter that bothered, but her family. She was afraid of their reaction when she showed up. Abby was glad Nate was with her, but what would he think when he realized how little her *dat* and *mam* regarded her? But then again their youngest daughter Clara was getting what she wanted, so maybe they would be in a good mood because of that. Perhaps they might even be warm and welcoming after not seeing her for over a month.

She sighed. Her stomach filled with painful butterflies as she closed her eyes and willed them to settle.

"I'm here, Abby," Nate said as if he'd somehow read her thoughts. He settled his hand briefly on her covered shoulder. "Everything will be *okey*."

With a smile, she nodded while attempting to stay positive. *"Ja."* She hoped so anyway.

The bus came to a stop, and Abby looked out the window. "Grove City," she murmured. "We are close." Her stomach flipped. *Too close.* About twenty minutes left to go.

"Look at me, Abby," Nate whispered loud enough for only her to hear.

She pulled her attention from the window to meet his gaze. His eyes were warm and caring. Staring into those brown orbs, she felt something settle inside of her. "I'm sorry."

He appeared surprised. "For what?"

"For…" She wasn't sure what to say.

"You're nervous. I understand that and think it's warranted." Nate's expression was soft and almost seemed loving. "Your *schweschter* wasn't nice to you when she visited."

Abby chuckled harshly. "I'm used to that, believe me. I don't know what her problem is. I didn't do anything to her. She's the one who…" *Received all our parents' love*, she thought.

"Who what?" he prompted.

She shook her head. "She's the baby." That was all she said, and his expression told her that he understood.

The bus stop in New Wilmington was in an area that Abby knew well. The bakery where she used to work was just a short walk down the street. The people at the bakery had always been nice and friendly—and good to her. She had called them last week to ask if they could give her and Nate a ride to the little inn in Amish country owned by the Palmers. She had reserved two rooms—one for Nate and one for her. The kind couple knew her well so they hadn't asked for a credit card number or a deposit. They understood she'd be good for the money.

She picked up her tote and Nate folded the blanket before storing it in his bag. "Follow me." Abby stepped off the bus to wait for the driver to take their luggage from under the vehicle. "We're heading to the bakery down the street. It's where I used to work. The owners are going to give us a ride to the inn."

Once they had their bags, she started toward the bakery. Nate paused on the sidewalk to peer at the desserts in the window. "This is where you worked?"

"One of the places," she said as she opened the door and preceded him inside.

"Abby!" Her former *English* employer June Rhodes smiled when she saw her. "It's wonderful to see you. You look well."

Abby grinned at the kind woman. "*Hallo*, June."

The woman's gaze settled on Nate next to her. "And this is the friend you said you'd be bringing?"

"This is Nate Hostetler," she replied. "He's my—"

"Betrothed," Nate interrupted with a smile. "Nice to meet you. Abby told me that she used to work here."

"Best employee we ever had," a man said as he entered from the back of the shop.

Abby grinned. "Jim."

"Young lady," he said with a smile. "So, I heard you need a ride to the Palmer B&B Inn."

"Yes, if you're sure you don't mind taking us," Abby said. "We'll pay you for your time."

"Of course, he'll take you," June said. "And you don't owe us anything. In fact—" She reached below the counter. When she straightened, she had an envelope in her hand, which she gave to Abby. "You never received your last paycheck."

Abby shook her head. "I left you in the lurch. I only gave you two days' notice."

"You worked harder than anyone I've ever known." Jim moved closer to his wife. "You don't owe us anything. We're the ones who are grateful we had you as long as we did." He nodded, and his wife pushed the money into Abby's hand.

"We added a little extra," June said.

Abby blinked back tears. "You were always nice to me." She sniffed. "You still are."

June shook her head. "That family of yours," she said with a growl. "You deserve better. Honestly, while we were sorry to see you go, we were glad for your sake that you were moving on. We hoped that people would be kinder to you where you ended up." She smiled at Nate. "I'm glad to see that that happened."

Abby gazed fondly at Nate. "I'm fortunate to have this man to support me through Clara's wedding."

"You make a cute couple," Jim said.

Blushing, Abby looked away.

"It's been a blessing for me that she moved to New Berne," Nate spoke up, surprising her. When she shot him a glance, he was smiling at her, his brown eyes filled with affection…and something more. If she didn't know better…she'd say it was love.

"Let me get my car keys, and then I'll take you." Jim left while she and Nate waited patiently with June.

Soon they would be checked into the Palmers' inn, a place close enough to walk to her parents' house. Now that the wedding was tomorrow, Abby felt more than a little nervous. Nate's hand on her lower back calmed her as they loaded their things into Jim's car, which he'd pulled up to the curb. She and Nate would have the rest of this day alone together, which was good. She needed to prepare him for her family and what their attitudes would be at the wedding.

As he drove them toward the inn, she and Jim talked about her new life in New Berne. "So, you'll be a schoolteacher," he said, sounding pleased. "You'll be a great one. You were always so good with the children who came into our bakery."

"She is wonderful with them," Nate replied, quick to speak up. "Our community is thrilled that she accepted the position. I'm more grateful than everyone else, and they are extremely appreciative."

"Nate!" Stunned, she could only stare at him. He seemed entirely sincere. Either he was a better actor than she could have imagined or he really felt that way. And wouldn't that be a blessing, for she had already developed genuine feelings for him.

Jim laughed. "Nate knows who he likes. You need to respect that in a man."

A moment later she heard the sedan's turn signal.

"We're here," her former employer exclaimed. He got out of the car and pulled their luggage from the trunk.

"Thank you, Jim."

"You're welcome. Call me if you need a ride when you're ready to leave, all right?" He waited, watchful, until she nodded. "Good." He extended his hand toward Nate. "I'm glad to meet you, young man. Take care of our girl here."

"I will," Nate said. "I promise."

"If you change your mind and want to leave before the wedding, give us a call. You can stay with us for a night or two, before you head home." Jim studied her as if he was worried about her.

"That's sweet of you, but I—we'll be fine," Abby reassured him. She watched Jim leave before she turned to Nate. "I guess we should check into our rooms."

Nate grinned as he nodded. "Then we can decide what to eat for supper."

Abby entered the inn first. "Mrs. Palmer?" she called when she didn't see the innkeeper.

"Call me Michelle. No need to be so formal," the woman said as she came from a back room. She grinned. "Why, it's Abby Yost! It's so good to see you. I'm glad that you made it here safely." She looked over at Nate. "And this is your young man?"

She nodded. "Yes. This is Nate Hostetler, my fiancé. Nate, this is Michelle Palmer, the owner."

"Nice to meet you," Nate said with a smile.

Michelle pulled out a guest book with a pen. "Please sign in." While Abby wrote their names in the book, the woman addressed Nate. "It's nice to see someone with Abby who cares about her."

"She's a wonderful woman," Nate replied. "I feel blessed to have her in my life."

"Thank you for arranging two rooms for us." Abby opened the envelope the Rhodeses had given her and pulled out twenty-dollar bills. There was more than enough to cover their stay.

"Put that money away, Abby. No need to pay me now. I've known you for years and I trust you," Michelle Palmer said. "How many times did you wait on me at Rhodes Bakery? Or at the general store?"

"A few, I guess." Abby couldn't help smiling at the cheerful woman.

"More than a few…" She went behind the counter and opened a cabinet where she withdrew two room keys. "You're on the second floor overlooking the backyard and farm," she told them. "Breakfast is from six until eleven. I planned on making you dinner since I knew you were arriving late."

"You don't have—" Abby started.

"I'm making meatloaf and baked potatoes, and there will be freshly grilled zucchini from our garden." Michelle smiled. "You must eat dinner with us. There'll be too much for just George and me."

Abby met Nate's gaze. "What do you think?"

"Sounds delicious to me." Nate flashed the innkeeper a smile. "Thank you."

"Oh, and I made a special pie for dessert." She handed them their keys. "Go on up to your rooms so you can rest and relax. There is plenty of time before supper. I figured we'd eat at six. Will that work for you?"

"It will." Abby glanced toward the stairs. "We'll take those stairs to our floor, Nate."

The woman smiled. "I left bottles of water and soda in your refrigerators. Please let me know if you need anything else."

"We will," Nate said.

They climbed the stairs to the second floor, where they easily found their rooms, located next to each other. Abby felt much better knowing that Nate would be close.

"Do you want to nap?" he asked as he unlocked his door with his key.

"Nay." After napping on the bus, she worried that if she slept again, she'd have trouble sleeping tonight. She already feared that anxiety would have her worrying too much about tomorrow to sleep well. Better to tire herself out so she could find a little sleep during the night.

"Let's grab sodas and enjoy them together," Nate suggested before he pushed his door open. "Oh, there is a balcony outside my room!"

"All the rooms at the back of the inn have balconies," Abby told him. "Which one will we use?"

"Yours." Nate grinned at her and disappeared inside his room to put down his things.

Abby already felt better at the prospect of his continued

company. She closed her eyes and prayed. "Please let things go *oll recht* tomorrow, Lord," she murmured.

She hated the realization that Nate would see firsthand how her family treated her.

Don't let him think less of me because of their poor behavior.

Chapter Fourteen

The wedding was being held at her parents' house. Usually, the ceremony would be elsewhere, but for some reason, Clara and Peter's exchange of vows as well as the couple's reception were to be at the same place. Abby viewed the hours ahead with dread. The morning of the wedding, she and Nate came downstairs early.

Michelle Palmer walked into the dining area with a smile. "Ready for breakfast?"

"Nate, you eat something," Abby said, "I'm not hungry." She was too nervous. Her stomach churned, her heart raced, and she felt on the verge of running far away from New Wilmington. *Wait*, she thought with sudden wry humor, *I already did*. Her home was in Lancaster County now. She gazed through the large windows to the beautiful scenery beyond.

"Are you *okey*?" Nate asked.

She shook her head. "*Nay*, but I will be." Abby managed a smile. "I appreciate you coming with me. It makes all the difference in the world."

It didn't take long for Nate to finish his meal. Unlike her, he must be hungry and not at all nervous, because he had no problem tucking into his food.

"What time do you have to be at the wedding?" Michelle asked as she collected plates and cups.

"Eight thirty," Abby said.

"An hour," the woman murmured. "Let us drop you off."

"It's not far." Abby stood and joined Nate as they prepared to return to their rooms. "I don't mind walking. I think the fresh air and exercise will do me good."

"I understand." Michelle picked up the tray of dishes and headed toward the kitchen. "Let me know if you need anything."

"We will," Nate answered. "Thank you."

"It was my pleasure." The innkeeper left, and Nate and Abby went up to their rooms for a short while to dress for the day's event.

When it was time to leave, Abby knocked on Nate's door. "Are you ready?" she asked.

He stepped out and locked his room behind him. She smiled at him when he faced her. Nate looked handsome in his Sunday best, consisting of a white shirt, a black vest and black trousers with a wide-brimmed black felt hat on his head. They left the inn and headed toward her family home. She was quiet as they walked side by side.

"I'm right here with you, Abby," Nate spoke up for the first time since they'd started toward her parents' house.

She stopped and waited until he looked at her. "I'm grateful that you offered to come with me, Nate. Today won't be easy for me. My family...seeing my *mam* and *dat*...and Clara with Peter."

"Do you still love him?" Nate asked. "Peter, I mean."

"Nay." She shook her head, knowing that it was true. She no longer cared for Peter. Even if he were free, she'd have nothing to do with him. But she still carried some hurt and anger over the way he'd treated her. He owed her an apology that she wasn't sure she'd ever get.

His wide smile made her light up inside. "I'll stay close to you if they let me."

Abby sighed. "It's hard to say what they'll do. I've given up trying to understand them. My parents have never supported me like they do my *schweschter.*"

The house was on the right. "There," she said, pointing to the place they had to go.

Buggies were pulling onto the lane to the house. She grabbed Nate's hand and was glad when he entwined their fingers. His grip bolstered her courage and self-esteem. He gave her hand a quick squeeze, and then they walked together toward the place where she used to live with her family.

Families climbed down from their wagons and buggies, dressed in their good clothes for the wedding. Some guests chatted as they walked up the driveway toward the house. A couple of friends said *hallo* to her, and she managed a smile as she returned their greeting.

Abby followed behind the others with Nate, taking the lane to the backyard where benches had been set up in rows under the shade of maple trees. Abby led Nate to one of the back rows. As she sat down, she wondered how long it would take for her sister and Peter to arrive. Her heart raced, and her hands felt clammy. She wished she was back in New Berne, where she'd felt happier than she'd ever been.

Soon the benches were filled with invited guests except for the first row. She caught sight of Mae Mast, the teacher she'd volunteered for, who waved at her from the far end of another row. The woman smiled, and Abby relaxed, happy that she was there. Then her anxiety returned, reaching an all-time high, as buggy wheels on the driveway made her look over. Her sister and Peter, the bride and the groom, had arrived.

She watched Peter emerge first from the buggy before

he reached in to help his bride. After she got out, Clara smiled widely at her groom, and the couple waited a moment as their attendants, Ruth Ann Yost—her and Clara's cousin—and Jake Graber—Peter's younger brother—got out of the vehicle and joined them.

As a group, the two couples walked to the front row of the congregation. Abby couldn't keep her gaze off Clara. Her sister looked lovely in a gown of light blue with a white apron and tucked-in cape. Her blond hair was pinned neatly under her white prayer *kapp*. Peter was taller than her and handsome in a black vest over a white shirt with black pants and shoes. His head was covered by a wide-brimmed black felt hat.

Abby saw her sister look over the guests as she followed her fiancé toward their seats. When Clara spotted her, satisfaction entered her expression but she didn't smile.

Abby tightened her fingers into fists on her lap. Why did Clara hate her so much? Abby had never done anything to her. It was Clara who had hurt her... Peter and Clara together. And her parents as well. Their only concern had been for their youngest daughter and her betrothed. Their refusal to acknowledge her feelings had wounded her most of all.

Nate covered one of Abby's fists, smoothing over her skin, his touch making her relax and open her fingers.

She met Nate's gaze, which was kind, warm and affectionate. She drew a deep, calming breath, smiled and then whispered, *"Danki."*

Nate understood Abby's pain and the awkwardness she was feeling as soon as Clara and Peter entered the backyard. He wondered why Abby's sister disliked her so much. After all, according to Abby, it was Clara who had hurt her after she'd charmed Peter away from her. Abby had done nothing wrong.

He glanced toward Abby and saw her gaze focused on her sister and her ex-betrothed. Had she been telling the truth earlier? Was she truly over him? If so, was there a chance that she might be ready to love again? Nate wanted a future with her, but they couldn't have one until they were both ready to let go of the past.

She seemed in a stupor as the ceremony droned on. He didn't like seeing her this way. Clearly, she was uncomfortable in her own home…her former home now.

Nate leaned close and whispered. "Do you want to leave?"

Abby blinked and met his gaze. She shook her head. "*Nay.* I'll be *oll recht.* If we don't stay for the meal, things will be worse for me with my family."

He nodded and took her hand, holding their linked fingers between them. Soon, but not soon enough for him, the wedding ceremony was over. It was quiet. Marriage was a serious business, so no one smiled or indicated good humor. If the people in this Amish community were happy for the couple, they didn't show it.

When the ceremony was over, guests rose from their seats and left. Abby didn't move. "The reception is inside the *haus,*" she said. "I'm not ready to go inside yet." After a minute, she drew a cleansing breath and finally stood. Nate immediately rose beside her. He watched as a woman came up to her, and he saw Abby's genuine smile for her.

"This is Mae Mast," Abby told him. "She's the teacher I volunteered for." She grinned at her friend. "Mae, this is Nate Hostettler, my fiancé."

"It's *wunderbor* to meet you, Nate," Mae said. The

teacher's husband gestured for her to join him, and the woman left.

"I'm glad I was able to meet your friend," Nate said as he gazed at her.

"I was happy to see her again." She glanced toward the house and sighed. "I guess we should head inside."

He placed his hand on her lower back. "I'm here, Abby." Nate felt warmth when her eyes shone at him with gratitude.

A few families were still standing outside as they approached the house. A man glanced at Abby, then quickly turned back to her with a surprised look. "Abigail," he greeted.

"*Onkel* Noah." She smiled. "It's so *gut* to see you. You're looking well."

"So are you." The older man frowned. "I didn't expect you to be here. Clara told Ruthie that you weren't coming."

"I don't know why she'd think that." Abby shifted closer to Nate who was there to speak up if she needed him to. "I told Clara I would be here."

"I'm glad you are. Your aunt and I haven't seen you in years." The man's gaze fell on Nate. "Who's your young man, Abby?"

Abby flashed him a smile that increased his heart rate. "This is Nathaniel Hostetler. Nate, this is my *onkel* Noah, my *vadder*'s *bruder*. His daughter Ruth Ann is Clara's attendant."

Nate nodded. He extended his hand. "Nice to meet you, Noah." The two men smiled as they clasped fingers and shook.

A woman stuck her head out the door. "Noah, come inside! Everyone is sitting down!"

"I'll be right in. I'm talking with Abigail," he told her, holding his wife's gaze.

"Abigail is here?" The woman stepped outside. "Abby, is that you?"

"*Ja*, it's me." Abby moved to where her aunt could see her. "*Hallo, Endie* Rosemary."

"*Hallo!*" Noah's wife smiled. "*Wunderbor!* Come inside. We can sit next to each other."

The next thing Nate knew they were seated in the back of the great room, the area having been expanded with the folding doors between the great room and the dining room open. Noah and Rosemary sat beside them, far away from the *Eck*, a U-shaped formation of tables in the front, where the newly married couple and their parents sat along with other immediate family members. Except Abby, he noted with a scowl. But Abby didn't seem to mind sitting with her aunt and uncle instead of at the *Eck*, so he decided he was fine with it.

It didn't seem to Nate as if there were many people there, but then he recalled that Abby had mentioned that this New Wilmington Amish community was much smaller than the one in New Berne. There were less than fifty people here, while back home he'd attended weddings with as many as two hundred in attendance.

The food served was a traditional Amish casserole, which was chicken with celery and stuffing. Sides of pepper slaw, fresh bread, buttered noodles, mashed potatoes, creamed celery, carrots and corn were also passed around for guests to enjoy. Celery was an important part of any reception feast, served in different ways and often used to decorate the tables in the same way that *Englishers* used flowers at their special events. Nate knew that after the main meal there would cakes and pies and other delicious deserts.

The food had been brought to the table before everyone had sat down. At the invitation of the newlyweds and Clara's parents, everyone started to pass dishes and fill up their plates.

Abby was quiet beside him, which worried him. He saw her occasionally interact with her aunt and uncle but that was it. He watched her carefully and saw her gaze settle more than once on the newlyweds up front and then move to her parents who sat not far from them and their attendants.

"Abigail," Rosemary said. "Are you happy in New Berne?"

"I am." Nate saw her warm smile, which delighted him. She locked gazes with him. "More than I expected to be." She paused and looked at her aunt. "Are you still living in Mount Gretna?" she asked.

Noah grinned at his niece. "We've recently moved back to New Wilmington."

"I see. To be closer to family, I suppose." Abby blinked and then chuckled. "This meal is delicious. You cooked it, didn't you, *Endie* Rosemary?"

Her aunt blushed. "Your *mudder* helped."

"She bought the ingredients and then had you do all the work." Abby shook her head. "I know better than to think *Mam* could cook anything remotely like this. She never had your talent."

"She never liked to cook." Noah forked up a mouthful of the chicken casserole. "My *frau* does…and I'm grateful." He shared a tender look with Rosemary.

"If you did all this work," Nate said, "why are you sitting back here with us?"

The woman shot him a wry smile. "My sister-in-law doesn't want anyone to know that I did all the cooking."

Abby released a heavy sigh that Nate felt deep inside him. So much pain, he thought, in such a young woman. Her parents never tried to seek her out or talk with her. How could they be that insensitive? Nate wondered. At least, she had a few people in New Wilmington who cared for her... the owners of the bakery and the bed-and-breakfast. And he was sure the teacher and students she'd helped while she lived here. And she had her aunt and uncle, now that they moved back in town. But except for Noah and Rosemary, who hadn't lived here until now, she'd had no other family who loved and appreciated her for the amazing woman that she was.

Once the main meal was done, the desserts came out next. "Did you make the sweets, too?" Abby asked Rosemary.

"*Nay*, she bought them at Rhodes Bakery," her aunt whispered so only the four of them could hear.

Abby laughed, and Nate thought the good humor only added to her loveliness.

"What's so funny?" her uncle asked.

Her green eyes twinkled. "I thought I recognized the strudel and cupcakes. I worked for June and Jim Rhodes at the bakery for years."

Noah chuckled. "Of course, you did." A plate of various desserts was handed to him, and he took pieces of two different cakes before he passed it to Nate.

"Knowing how much she dislikes your *eldre*, do you think June did something to these?" Nate whispered in her ear teasingly.

Abby giggled but shook her head. "She wouldn't do that." She bit her lip. "June knew I'd be attending."

Clara rose from her chair and started in their direction, and Nate murmured softly, "Your *schweschter* is headed our way."

Abby nodded. "I see her. Be prepared for her worst."

The bride came to stand behind them. Abby turned so that she could meet her sister eye to eye.

"So, I see you came," Clara said. "I'm surprised that you brought the builder with you."

"Excuse me?" Abby said. "I brought the man I love, and I don't know why that would surprise you. Jake at the general store promised to tell you to add him as my plus-one when I called, and he's never made a promise he didn't keep."

Clara seemed taken aback. "The man you…"

"Love, *ja*." Abby appeared angry on his behalf.

Clara's gaze moved to Nate and she appeared to take him in anew and then dismiss him in the span of seconds.

"Is it so hard to believe that your *schweschter* has found happiness outside of New Wilmington?" Nate was upset but he appreciated Abby sticking up for him. He was falling for her, and he wished what she'd just told Clara was true and not part of the arrangement they'd agreed upon.

Then to his amazement, Clara backed down. Her expression softened as she eyed Abby as if she was no longer a threat to her and her new husband. "I'm…happy for you, Abigail. Truly."

Abby, true to her sweet nature, smiled warmly at Clara. "*Danki*. I'm happy for you, too."

Clara spoke briefly with her aunt and uncle then headed back to her table.

"She loves him," Abby murmured to Nate as she watched her sister walk away. "She honestly loves him."

"Looks like it." Nate grinned. "Will wonders never cease. *Gott* works in mysterious ways, *ja*?" He ate a bit of chocolate cake, and she laughed.

The sound of her laughter shivered along his spine and captured his heart the rest of way. He saw him and Abby happily living together on a dairy farm. Maybe they could have that future…when he worked up the courage to ask Abby if they could make their relationship real. He liked her but he didn't want to rush into anything, like he had with Emily. And Abby was still working through feelings of her own.

"Ach nay!" Abby breathed. He could sense her tense up.

"What is it?" he asked with concern.

"Now Peter is coming this way."

He looked over and watched as the groom moved in their direction without Clara. Nate reached for her hand under the table and held on to it. He stared at the man while concealing dislike. How could Peter have discarded Abby, a sweet woman who was kind and generous, the way he had? Nate certainly wouldn't make the same mistake.

Chapter Fifteen

"Abigail," Peter greeted as he stood near her chair.

She glanced back at him. "*Hallo*, Peter." So much had changed since she'd last seen him. She couldn't believe she had once loved him and thought she would marry him. He was so different from the man sitting next to her. Her face warmed as Nate squeezed her hand under the table, a clear show of allyship.

"*Danki* for coming," he said. "Clara and I appreciate it."

"Clara didn't give me much choice," she said with a sad smile. She wasn't bitter, just unhappy that she had to be coerced into attending.

She saw him wince. "I… Can I speak with you a moment?" She saw him look at Nate. "In private?"

Abby shook her head. "Anything you have to say to me can be said in front of Nate."

Peter nodded but didn't look thrilled. "Let's go outside for a minute."

She and Nate followed Peter out into the side yard. She waited until her sister's husband halted and faced them.

"What did you need to talk to me about?" she asked, waiting patiently. With Nate by her side, she felt supported and cherished.

"I…" Her ex-betrothed shifted uncomfortably. "I wanted—

needed—to apologize to you. For what happened between Clara and me. You're a fine young woman, and you deserved better."

"I can't argue with that," Nate said as he moved closer to her side.

Peter scowled, and Abby had to stifle a laugh. Nate's comment only made her affection for him grow. She was grateful for him and this arrangement they'd made...even if she secretly wanted it to be real.

Finally, her new brother-in-law sighed. "He's *recht*. I led you to believe we could have a life together and then I threw it away when I got involved with your *schweschter* behind your back."

"What are you apologizing for, Peter?" she asked. "For throwing me away or for getting involved with me in the first place?"

"I never meant to hurt you, Abigail," he said with a sincerity she couldn't deny. "You know that I lost my wife and unborn child. I wanted to marry again and to have children." He paused. "I knew you'd be a wonderful wife and mother, and that was what was most important to me at the time. But then I met Clara...and she became what was most important to me."

"I understand." She flashed a smile at Nate. "*Danki* for your apology. I believe that everything turned out the way *Gott* wanted. I moved to New Berne, and Nate and I found each other."

Peter blinked. "You and he are betrothed?"

"We are," Nate piped up. "Abby is amazing. I couldn't help but fall in love with her."

"Abby?" Peter asked as if he'd never heard the nickname before.

"*Ja*, Abby. Abigail is too formal for what she and I have

together." Nate gazed at her with an affection that seemed all too real.

"I'm happy for you." Peter smiled. "We both have what we want—someone we love with a forever future. And with children."

Abby studied him for a long moment. It suddenly occurred to her why they had moved up Peter and Clara's wedding from August to July. "Why the rush to get married?"

Peter shifted uncomfortably. "There isn't a rush. I love Clara, Abigail, and she loves me. We are eager to start our life together and have a family. I recently bought a place far outside of New Wilmington, and I'd wanted her with me when I move."

Abby nodded. "And you never felt that way about me," she said softly.

The man she used to love blushed a bright red. "I'm sorry I hurt you," he said in a hoarse voice. "I know I should have told you sooner about me and Clara. It wasn't *recht* for us to meet in secret."

"It wasn't," she agreed. "But it's *oll recht*." She smiled. "Be happy with my *schweschter*, Peter. I have already forgiven you."

She felt the warmth of Nate's hand on her lower back, soothing her.

Abby gave him a small smile. "All is *gut*, Peter. You should get back to your bride. I've already made my peace with her. Enjoy this day and your happily-ever-after."

His expression softened. "*Danki*...Abby."

"Abigail to you," Nate said with a growl.

Her sister's husband gave Nate a slow nod, then quickly went back inside, leaving her and Nate alone.

"You shouldn't have had to talk with him," Nate said

with brown eyes filled with warmth. "But, at least, he finally apologized although he should have done it sooner."

"It's fine. I'm *oll recht* with them… It's my *eldre* I'm having a hard time understanding. They never gave a thought to what I felt when Peter and Clara got together. And they haven't spoken to me since I arrived." Why didn't they love her as much as they love Clara? Abby gazed at Nate and found a comfort in his presence that helped ease the pain of her parents' neglect. She had a new life in a new place with people who cared about her. That was what really mattered. "I guess we should go back inside. I should say *hallo* to my *mam* and *dat* before we leave."

"Are you ready to go?" Nate fell into step beside her, his hand still on her spine.

"Not yet. I'll let you know when it's time." She grinned at him. "Then we can head back to the Palmers and enjoy the rest of our stay with them. *Ja?*"

"Sounds *gut* to me." He opened the door for her and she preceded him inside.

The first person she saw as they entered the kitchen was her mother. "Where have you been, Abigail?" she snapped. "This is your *schweschter*'s special day."

"Nate and I were taking a breather outside. The weather is lovely." She looked at Nate for support.

He quickly stepped up to the plate. "*Ja*, it is beautiful outside. How wise of you to hold the ceremony in the backyard." He smiled. "I'm Nate Hostetler," he said, "Abby's fiancé."

"Her fiancé?" her mother echoed while raising her eyebrows.

"*Ja*, my fiancé…my betrothed." Then, having had enough of being treated poorly by her mother, Abby brushed by her and returned to the reception. The problem was with her mother, not her, she decided. It hurt knowing that, but at least she had people in her life now who made her feel valued and worthy.

Nate watched Abby as she wove her way through the room. He was proud of the way Abby had held her own. She'd listened to Peter and then forgiven him…and she'd made peace with her sister. Her kindness and understanding only made him admire her more.

"Would you like coffee?" she asked as she reached their table again.

"*Ja*, but I can get it." He beamed at her.

"I'll bring it to you," Abby said. "After all, that's what a woman does for her intended."

His chest tightened at her words. She chuckled and went to get him a cup of coffee. He watched her go, wanting to protect her from her family and show her how much she deserved to be treated well. But those feelings had no place in this situation. Today had already been so difficult for her—he would wait until another time to share the depth of his feelings for her. For now, he pushed those thoughts aside and focused on enjoying this day with her.

When she returned and set his coffee before him, he grinned at her. "I thought I'd eat more dessert. What can you recommend?"

"June's apple pie is *wunderbor*. Why don't you try that?" She appeared amused. "If you want something chocolate, try her brownies. They're delicious! She uses big chocolate chunks with a top layer of light creamy chocolate frosting."

He widened his eyes. "I'll take a sampling of both."

As he reached the plate of treats on the table, Abby leaned to whisper. "There's my *dat*. I'm going to visit with him."

Nate nodded, while hoping that she wouldn't be hurt

by another family member. He watched her as he took a bite from a brownie. Her mother wasn't at the table. Abby reached the chair close to her father and sat down. The man looked surprised when he saw his daughter. When her *dat* broke out in a smile for Abby, Nate was relieved. He filled his plate and went back to the corner of the room where he and Abby had been seated.

Abby's uncle was just returning to his chair with a cup in his hand as Nate approached. Nate offered him the dessert plate, and Noah took a piece of cinnamon coffee cake.

"May I ask you something?" Nate asked. When Noah nodded, he continued, "I know it isn't my place to ask, but I'd like to know. Is there a reason Abby's mother treats Abby differently from Clara?" Her father looked as if he cared when she went over to talk with him. "Her *dat* seems to love her."

Noah looked pained. "I don't know if I should tell you."

"Why not?" He studied the man. "You can trust me. Abby and I are betrothed." So, it was a fake betrothal, but he hoped that someday, they might make it real. And in the meantime, he and she were close friends, weren't they? He understood this was a delicate topic, and maybe he had no right to ask. But if it would help Abby, he wanted to know.

"It's a sad story, and Abby doesn't know about it." Noah checked his surroundings and then turned in his seat to face Nate. "Abby is my niece, but although he loves her, my *bruder* Matthew is not her father."

Frowning, Nate asked. "He's not?"

"Nay." He looked about him again as if nervous that someone would overhear.

"Would you rather talk outside?" Nate said.

The man shook his head. "I'll make this quick. Abby's father was my older *bruder* Abram. He and his wife, Cath-

erine—Abby's mother—were killed in a terrible buggy accident after a car struck them head-on. Abby was only a
baby when it happened. She was in the vehicle with them
but because of a special wooden seat her father had made
for her, by the grace of our Lord, she survived."

Nate waited patiently for him to continue.

"When he and Dorothy took her in to raise her as their
own, Matthew thought it best that Abby never learn about
the accident or her parents." He took another quick look
around before he continued. "Dorothy understood Abby
needed her and was willing to be a mother to her. While
she cared for Abby, she discovered she was pregnant." He
paused. "She lost her unborn baby at five months along.
The child would have been their *soohn* if he'd lived. Dorothy blamed Abby for her miscarriage despite the doctor's
assurance that there were problems with the baby. The boy
wouldn't have survived even if he'd made it to full term.
Abby hadn't caused the miscarriage, nature had. Unfortu-
nately, Dorothy needed someone to blame and she chose
Abby. She got pregnant again and gave birth to a girl. Clara.
She never had the little boy she always wanted."

"I'm sorry to hear all this," Nate said sincerely. His heart
ached for the whole family. "Still, to blame a little girl
wasn't right."

"I agree, but we weren't here to see it, so we weren't
able to interfere. From what I've been told, things became
tense after the miscarriage but everything truly changed
for Abby after Clara was born. The baby was of Dorothy's
blood and to Dorothy, that meant she was somehow better
than poor Abby. We had no idea until the next time we visited. And there was nothing we could do." Noah went silent
when his wife approached the table but then she stopped to
talk with another guest. "We were allowed to bring Abby

home with us for a visit, but Matthew loved Abby and wanted her back, despite knowing that his wife wasn't the mother she should have been for her. We should have kept her. My wife and I regret we didn't try harder to convince Matthew to let us have her."

"I understand," Nate said. "I appreciate you telling me."

Noah nodded. "I was glad when I heard that Abigail moved to New Berne to take a teaching position." His gaze went to Abby, who was visiting with her father. "Matthew loves her, but he lets Dorothy have her own way in most things, and since the miscarriage Dorothy has never accepted her. I frankly don't think she wanted Abby at all. Now that you're in Abigail's life, things will get better for her."

Nate started to speak but saw the aunt approaching and took a bite of cake.

Rosemary returned to the seat next to her husband. Nate smiled at her and then focused his attention on Abby. He saw a young woman stop to talk briefly with her. Her cousin Ruth, he remembered. Noah's daughter. Dorothy returned to the table where Abby's father sat and must have said something disparaging to Abby, because Abby quickly got up and left, before the woman took back her seat.

Abby walked back to Nate but remained standing. "I'm ready to leave when you are."

"I'm ready." Nate stood. "It was nice meeting both of you, Noah and Rosemary."

As Nate rose, he listened to Abby thanking her aunt and uncle for their company.

"Have a safe trip home, Abigail," Noah said.

Her smile for him was genuine. "Enjoy living in New Wilmington."

Then he and Abby left together by the back entrance.

They walked down the lane in silence and started toward the Palmers' inn.

"Are you *oll recht*?" he asked her finally.

She shook her head. "*Nay*, but I will be." When she reached to grasp his hand, he was grateful.

"That girl who spoke to you just before we left," Nate said as they walked back, hand in hand, to where they were staying. "That was your cousin Ruth, *ja*? Clara's attendant?"

"*Ja*. She didn't understand why Clara asked her instead of me." Abby sighed heavily. "She was told I wouldn't be at the wedding and that was the reason."

Noah gave her fingers a little squeeze in comfort and then he continued to hold her hand until they reached the inn.

As soon as they stepped into the bed-and-breakfast, Nate felt surrounded by caring people who clearly loved Abby.

"How was the wedding?" Michelle greeted from the reception desk, her gaze sharp, as she studied Abby.

"Interesting," Nate said while Abby simply shrugged her shoulders. It seemed that the woman understood that not much had changed for Abby with her family.

"Would you like to sit on the patio?" Michelle asked. "Jim and I will be happy to join you for a while. I have freshly squeezed lemonade."

"You don't need to stay here at the desk?" Abby asked.

"No. Someone will ring the bell if they need me." Michelle pointed out.

Abby gave her a genuine smile. "Sounds wonderful, then!" She turned to him. "Nate?"

"I'm all for lemonade and a nice, relaxing chair outdoors," he said.

Within minutes, they were seated in comfortable, cushioned lounge chairs with a view of the backyard and the farmland beyond.

Nate grew thoughtful as he enjoyed the conversation between Abby and the Palmers. He was glad to see Abby in better spirits after what had been a trying day.

Now that Noah had confessed the truth to him about Abby's parents and the past, Nate struggled with whether to tell her. He decided that he would wait until they got back to New Berne and could find the right time and place, if he chose to tell her at all. But how could he not?

He feared the news might upset her...and make her angry with the messenger. Nate feared that she'd be hurt if he told her, but did he have the right to keep it from her? Keeping secrets wasn't the best way to treat a friend...much less a friend he wanted more with.

After offering up another prayer to *Gott*, he forced it from his mind. He would continue to seek the Lord's guidance until he could figure what to do.

Chapter Sixteen

Abby knew it was going to be difficult for her to say good-bye to Michelle Palmer and her husband. She loved these people and would miss them. "If you ever get a vacation, please come to New Berne," she said, ready to insist on paying their bill.

Michelle looked sad. "We may have to figure out a way to do that."

Nate stood at Abby's side, their packed bags on the floor by their feet. She felt his support even then, knowing that she wanted to see them again but it might not happen.

"I can tell what you're thinking, Abby Yost," the inn-keeper told her. "And I'm not charging you for your rooms."

Abby shook her head. "No, Michelle! It's not fair for us to stay here for free."

"Abby, you came through for me when I desperately needed help, and you refused to let me pay you." Determined, Michelle folded her arms across her chest. She addressed Nate. "I met Abby when she worked at the bakery. One day, when I went in to purchase muffins, Abby could see that I was upset. We had a lot of guests check out that morning, and we'd booked a full house for the next day." She smiled at Abby. "This young woman asked me what was wrong, and I told her. The girls who cleaned rooms for me were sick, and I was at a loss about what to do. Abby commiserated with me and made me feel better for venting. Then an hour later, she showed up at the inn. She said she was ready to clean rooms for me. Because of her, everything was ready for the arrival of our guests." The woman's gaze went back and forth from Nate to her. "She saved me that day, said she wanted to help a friend who needed her. And that wasn't the only time Abby stepped in to make things easier for me."

Michelle unfolded her arms. "Abby, you will not pay for your rooms. I owe you more than a couple of free rooms. Do you understand?"

Abby blushed, aware of Nate's regard. "I do."

"Good!" Michelle said, satisfied. "George will take you to the bus station. George!"

The woman's kind husband appeared with a smile. "All set?" he asked. "No rush."

"We're ready," Abby said and took stock of her surroundings one last time. She had enjoyed her stay here and was grateful she'd been able to spend time with the Palmers again.

"Take these," Michelle said. "Sandwiches, snacks and water for the ride home."

Abby opened her mouth to object, but then changed her mind. "Thank you." She stuffed them in her tote and slipped the strap over her shoulder. Then she bent to pick up her suitcase.

Nate reached for it before she could reach it. "I'll take that."

"Nate," she warned.

He smirked at her. "Just go to the car, Abby."

She sighed. "Fine." She heard Michelle chuckle behind her as she and Nate followed George to his vehicle. Abby waited until their bags were in the trunk before she turned back with tears in her eyes. "Michelle, thank you for everything," she murmured, feeling emotional. If not for the Palmers and the Rhodeses along with the Amish community teacher and the students at the school where she'd volunteered to work, living in New Wilmington for as long as she had would have been unbearable.

Michelle gave her a hug. "Safe travels."

Abby nodded and then her gaze sought Nate's as she slid into the car. The warmth in his brown eyes made her feel instantly better.

The drive to the bus stop didn't take long. "I'll miss you and Michelle," she told George.

The older man smiled. "We'll miss you. Come see us again." Then he left them to wait for their ride.

The bus arrived fifteen minutes later. Soon, she and Nate were seated side by side, ready for the long journey home.

Nate enjoyed the passing scenery outside the bus. It was interesting in places and quite beautiful in others. He saw lawns and trees rich with summer's green. Bright flowers added a dash of color, immediately drawing his eye. Wildflowers lined the grass median on the highway and along the edges of the road. Intentional plantings of zinnias, vincas and knockout roses brought life to gardens in homes and business properties in many of the towns they traveled through.

When they first got onto the bus, Nate had urged Abby to take the window seat so that she could enjoy the view. He was worried about her. She gazed out the window silently, and he understood that she was suffering from mixed feelings after her time back in New Wilmington. He'd felt the depth of her emotional struggle to leave the people who'd been kind to her—the Rhodeses and the Palmers. And at the wedding, her aunt, uncle and cousin. She was silent for so long that he leaned over to check on her.

"Abby," he murmured, not wanting to wake her if she was asleep. She had closed her eyes, but he couldn't tell if she was resting or out like a light.

When she didn't respond, he sighed with relief. He knew the visit had been hard on her, despite the improvement in the interaction with her sister and Clara's new husband. Her aunt and uncle had been nice people.

Thoughts of Noah and what he'd revealed to him made him uneasy. He still couldn't decide whether her uncles were right or wrong in keeping her past a secret from her. Abby had suffered needlessly over the years, wondering why her parents didn't love her like they did Clara. Now that he knew the truth, he had to think long and hard if telling her would help her understand or hurt her more.

He watched over her beside him. It wasn't overly cold in the bus. If it became chilly, he'd cover her with a blanket like he had the other day. All he wanted was to take care of her and make her happy. Abby Yost was a beautiful woman inside and out, and he loved her. What would happen if he confessed what he'd learned? Would she be angry with him? Would it ruin all his chances to have a future with her?

Abby woke up with a start. She seemed to settle when she saw him seated beside her. "How long have I been asleep?"

"About three hours." Nate gazed at her with tenderness welling inside him.

She looked alarmed. "*Nay*, it couldn't have been that long."

He chuckled. "We have two hours or a little longer until we get home."

"I'm so sorry I fell asleep on you," she said.

"You fell asleep against the window," he teased. "You haven't been sleeping well the last two nights. You deserve to rest, Abby."

"I...*nay*, I haven't gotten much sleep since two days before we left for the wedding." She straightened in her seat and stretched. "*Danki* again for going with me, Nate."

"No need to thank me. It was my pleasure." He reached for her bag under the seat before him and unzipped it. "Want a water or snack? You didn't eat much this morning."

She shrugged. "I'll take a water. I'm still not hungry, but if there is something sweet in that bag, I'll try to nibble on that."

Nate pulled out two chocolate bars and bag of cookies. "Which one?"

"Both," she said, which made him laugh. "What?"

"I'm still not hungry," he mimicked.

Her lips twitched in response. "*Okey*, so I'm hungry for sweets." She grinned when he handed her the chocolate bar and placed the cookies between them.

The ride seemed to go quicker after that. Nate figured that there were about a half hour away from home when Abby turned in her seat to face him.

"Nate?"

He recognized a shift in her demeanor. She sounded as if she needed to talk about something weighing on her mind. "*Ja?*"

She seemed hesitant before she continued. "Now that the wedding is over, what happens to our fake relationship?"

Nate couldn't get a good read on her thoughts. "Why? Are you in a hurry to break up with me?"

"Nay!" Her quick denial gave him hope.

"Let's leave things as they are for now," he said. "Everyone in our community believes we are betrothed. No need for them to think we weren't serious about each other, especially after just returning from a trip together." Even as he said the words, he knew it was an excuse. He wanted to ask her to go out with him for real.

Her face fell as if she was disappointed in his answer. *"Ach,* I forgot about that. It makes sense to continue as we have been."

"Besides, we've become close friends, *ja*?" he pushed, hoping for a sign she wanted more.

Her green eyes brightened. *"Ja,* we have."

"I want to talk about this tomorrow." Nate couldn't keep his eyes off her. Her green dress did wonders for her eyes and hair, highlighting both as if making her glow. But then she always looked wonderful to him. "I'd like to spend a lot more time together, in case Emily comes for a visit." It was just an excuse and a poor one.

She bobbed her head. "I agree."

Warmth combined with relief settled in his chest at the prospect of having the time to win her heart. There were times he thought she might care for him, too, but he wasn't certain. The idea of her loving him hovered for a long moment, giving him hope.

"What are your plans for when you get home?" Abby's gaze connected to his and he captured it for as long as she allowed him.

"After a day of rest, I'll be working on the *schule*. I need to paint the classroom." He cocked his head as he studied her. "What about you?"

"Same, except I'll be checking in with Jonas about the

order for primers, textbooks and other supplies for my students. And I need to work on lesson plans."

"Then I'd better get those bookshelves done soon, too," he said with a smile.

"*Ja*, you better," she replied sternly. And then she laughed.

The bus arrived in New Berne at two thirty in the afternoon. While Abby had slept, Nate had called Jonas for a ride.

As expected, Jonas was waiting for them in the parking lot near the bus stop.

"Is that Jonas?" Abby asked before they got off the bus.

"*Ja*," he said. "He'll be taking us to my place and I'll take you home from there."

Nate noted Abby's surprise when he asked her to come into his house after Jonas dropped them off. "Let's just take a few moments and relax, *ja*?" he said.

He heard her release a sharp breath as he pulled out a chair for her.

"*Okey.*" She sat down and looked around the kitchen. "Homey." Abby appeared exhausted despite the nap she had on the bus. He wouldn't keep her long.

He smiled. "I'll take you home in a few minutes." He was relieved to see that her smile in response looked genuine though small.

Nate went to his refrigerator and poured two glasses of cold tea. He handed her one. "Here. You've barely had anything to eat or drink today." He watched with satisfaction as she took a sip. "First, how are you? Be honest."

Abby took another swallow before answering. "I'm fine. I admit it was a hard time for me, but you made it easier. Having you there was everything I needed to get through the wedding and the visit."

"I know you want to see the Palmers again," he said. "We could go back to see them."

She shook her head. "I don't think that's a *gut* idea. If the inn was any place else, I'd consider it, but...it's too close to my parents'."

Nate studied her, noting her distress. "I understand. But if you decide at another time that you'd like to go, please keep me in mind for the trip."

Abby seemed stunned by his offer. "You'd go with me all that way again?"

He inclined his head. "I would."

"Why? Why would you do that for me?" She gazed at him with an intensity that took him by surprise.

He smiled. "Because I care for you."

Chapter Seventeen

"He said he cares for me," Abby murmured with excitement as she walked from room to room in her cottage a short time later after she got home. "Did he mean it?" Had he said it because he felt sorry for her after meeting the disaster that was her family? Or did he mean he cared for her as a friend?

When he'd dropped her off yesterday afternoon, Nate had reminded her that he wasn't going to work today, that they could spend the day together. What were his plans for them? He'd never told her. She knew he wanted to keep up the appearance of a relationship in their community for a while because of Emily, but she and her husband were gone and not due for a visit anytime soon. Despite what he'd said, it wasn't necessary to stay betrothed because of them. He and she would have to break up eventually, which she dreaded.

Abby frowned. She didn't think much of Emily. She didn't like that Emily allowed him to court her and then rejected his marriage proposal.

Nate was kind and sweet. He was everything she'd ever wanted in a man. The thought that their relationship—fake or not—would eventually end upset her. And much more than a little.

She paused in an open doorway and closed her eyes briefly. She didn't want just friendship with him. Abby wanted everything. Her cottage and its contents made her constantly think of Nate. The craftsmanship of his work… the way he'd been eager for her to see the finished cottage and then his excitement to show it to her again after the furniture was in place. She chuckled, remembering how happy he was with her reaction to her new home.

I love Nate. And she had for some time, she realized. She'd never been treated so well by anyone until him. The way he supported her on the trip, the little things he did to take care of her, like making sure she slept and ate. Everything he'd done had made her feel special, and she'd found herself smiling even while they were in New Wilmington. She'd never had anyone like that in her life before. While her relationship with Peter had been exciting at first, she realized now that Peter had never been as considerate and caring toward her as Nate was. She'd been flattered when Peter had stopped by to see her wherever she'd been working. Abby had enjoyed his visits, but compared to Nate, her ex had never been concerned with what she thought or how she felt. He'd liked that she was by nature a hard worker, but did Peter worry about her? Support her? *Nay.*

Nate continued to show concern for her, and he worried about her, seeming to know what she wanted or needed. Abby realized that she should have had a clue within weeks that Peter wasn't right man for her. Even before he'd secretly begun seeing her sister behind her back.

Abby trusted Nate to be completely honest with her. Moving into the living room, she sat in a chair and closed her eyes. He'd told her that he wouldn't lie or keep secrets from her.

She had no idea what time Nate would stop by. Would

they enjoy hot dogs at the outdoor stand again? Go for ice cream? Take a walk? Did he have anything specific in mind for them to do?

Could Nate possibly return her feelings? If he didn't, she knew the pain of his rejection would hurt far worse than her sadness about her breakup with Peter.

A knock on the back door drew her attention and she hurried to answer it. She grinned when she caught the bright smile on Nate's handsome face. "*Gut mariga*, Nate!"

He beamed at her as he studied her. "What a pretty, blue dress! You look *wunderbor*." He couldn't seem to take his eyes off her and her face warmed at the thought.

"*Danki.*" She was glad she had chosen to wear her short-sleeved, light-blue garment. The color did something different and flattering to her complexion and her eyes. "You look handsome as always. I love the color of your shirt... like cranberries." He wore short sleeves in that bright shade of berry red. The pants he had on were navy denim triblend trousers, held up by straw-colored suspenders that seemed to match the wide-brimmed, black-banded straw hat on his head.

He chuckled. "A shirt color like fruit," he said with amusement but he seemed pleased by what she'd said. Finally, he gestured toward his buggy behind him. "Are you ready to take a ride with me?"

She blinked. "Where are we going?"

"It's a surprise." He stepped back to allow her to exit the cottage and lock it behind her. He opened his buggy door and helped her inside.

"Such a kind, thoughtful man," she said with a smile.

Nate took her to a wide, grassy area where sunlight dappled on the rippling water of a pond. There were a few trees growing close by. There were swing sets to the far left and what looked like a hiking trail beyond the playground. Picnic tables and brightly colored benches were situated in different areas for visitors to use and enjoy.

"Welcome to our New Berne Community Park," he said with a smile.

Abby glanced around with delight. "It's beautiful here," she said softly.

"It is." When she looked at him, she found that he was gazing at her and not at the park or the water.

"Nate," she whispered, unable to turn away from him.

"There's a place to sit." He broke her gaze and gestured toward a vibrant blue metal bench in the shade of a single oak tree. "Let's try it out."

She nodded and followed him to the bench. He checked to ensure it was clean before he sat and patted the seat beside him, and she was touched by the gesture. "I didn't know this existed," she said.

"You haven't had a proper tour of New Berne yet." He stared at the pond, as if entranced. "There is something I want to talk with you about."

"Okey." A pleasant breeze caressed her face and exposed skin. "What is it?"

"It's about our trip and the wedding." Something in his tone brought her attention to his expression. He appeared nervous, anxious. She couldn't figure out why.

Abby wasn't sure she wanted to hear what he had to say. She wasn't sure why she felt that way, but she felt a pit in her stomach and a shiver along her nape down her spine that told her what he was about to say would change everything.

She was beautiful in her blue dress, but then Abby always appealed to him no matter what she wore. Gazing into her pretty, green eyes, Nate felt sick to his stomach. He cared for Abby so much—he was in love with her—and he was afraid to tell her what he knew about her family. But on the other hand, she trusted him not to lie or keep things hidden from her. Like her ex-fiancé had.

"Nate? What do you want to tell me?" She appeared worried...and he could see that she was afraid of what he had to say.

I must tell her. He could only hope she wouldn't be angry with him. He breathed deeply and then released a sigh. "When you went to visit your *vadder*, your *onkel* Noah told me something. It's something I think you'd want to know." He stared down at his lap while trying to find the right words.

He continued, "First, I need to tell you that I think you are an amazing woman, and despite your childhood and the unhappiness you endured at home and after Peter's betrayal, you deserve only the best things that life has to offer."

Her brow creased. "You're scaring me, Nate," she said, hugging herself with her arms.

He lifted his gaze to her. "I don't mean to. It's just that this is a delicate matter. I was told it would be better if I kept it from you, but I don't think it's fair or true."

"What is it?" she whispered.

Heart beating wildly, Nate continued, "You once commented that your *eldre* have always favored your younger *schweschter.*"

"*Ja*, it's true. I have always felt that they love Clara more than me," she admitted, her tone and expression laced with pain.

"Have you ever wondered why a mother...or a father would be so obvious in affection for one child over another?" Nate placed his hand on her arm, soothing her enough to watch her move hands to her lap.

"When I was younger I thought it was because I wasn't as pretty as Clara," she began. "I worked hard all the time… inside and outside our *haus*. But then I realized that I only felt that way because of my mother."

He nodded. "First, you are far prettier than Clara. I think you're beautiful inside and out. As for your working hard all the time, I would know that to be true even if you hadn't told me that, based on comments made by June Rhodes and Michelle Palmer when we were with them." He turned in his seat to face fully. "What both women said that made me think long and hard about why a woman as generous and warm as you should have suffered at the hands of her own family."

He paused and covered her hands with his. "You're beautiful and sweet, a truly lovely young woman." Nate hesitated, afraid. "At the wedding, while you were visiting with your *dat*, I asked Noah why your parents clearly treat you differently than they do Clara. And do you know what he said?"

"What?" It was clear to him that she was nervous and fearful about learning the truth.

"That Dorothy and Matthew aren't your real parents," he began, wishing he could hold her close as he continued.

"What?" She gaped at him in disbelief.

"It's true," he said softly. "They are your *endie* and *onkel* like Noah and Rosemary are. Your *dat* and *mam* were killed in a buggy accident after a car hit them and ran the vehicle off the road. Their names were Abram and Catherine Yost. Abram was Matthew and Noah's older *bruder*. You were just a baby, strapped onto the back bench of the buggy in a wooden seat your father made to keep you safe. Thankfully, you were unharmed. Dorothy and Matthew took you in…and Matthew loved you and wanted to raise his *bruder*'s *dochter*."

"What happened? Did I do something terrible? Is that why my m—aunt never loved me?" The aching tone of her voice made him want to cry and reach out to hold her tightly.

"*Nay.* You did nothing wrong," Nate assured her. "Noah said that Dorothy was with child when they took you in, but she didn't know it yet. It wasn't until she miscarried that everything changed for Dorothy. Matthew still cared for you, but he wouldn't go against his wife, and he, as well as Dorothy, were grieving for the child they lost."

Abby glanced at him with devastation in her beautiful green eyes. "But why would that change how they felt about me? I don't understand."

He hesitated. How do you tell the woman you loved more than anyone and anything that the person she thought of as her mother had blamed a toddler for the death of her infant? Blamed her. Even though she'd had nothing to do with the miscarriage. "Abby—"

"Tell me," she exploded. "Tell me now!"

"I… I think Noah was *recht* to keep this a secret." Nate saw her pain and didn't know how to help her. He wished he'd kept silent so she wouldn't suffer. "I thought knowing would bring understanding, but I was wrong."

"You thought I should know, so tell me!" Abby was getting irate. Nate had never seen her this angry before.

"Dorothy…your *endie*…the woman you thought was your *mudder*… She needed someone to blame for the death of her unborn *soohn*." He reached for her hand and held it. "You. I'm so sorry, but she blamed you."

"How did I survive in that *haus* if no one wanted me,

when they never loved or cared for me?" Tears filled her eyes. *"How?"*

"Dorothy was upset, but Matthew genuinely loved you," Nate said. He slipped his arm behind her on the bench but she jerked away and stood as if eager to put distance between her and him. His spirits sank as he realized that he might have just ruined their relationship and his hope for a future with her.

"Will you take me home?" she asked, staring off into space. When he didn't immediately reply, she faced him, her expression hard. "Nathaniel, I want to go home."

Nate stood as she did, upset by the heartrending change in her. "I'll take you." He trailed behind as she hurried to his buggy as if she couldn't wait to be as far away from him as she could get.

She remained silent as he drove the buggy back to the cottage. She never said a word as she got out before he had a chance to climb down and help her.

"Abby! Let me go inside with you. *Please*," he called, desperate to ease her pain. "Maybe I can help. I hate that you're hurting."

"Nay, Nate," she said without looking at him. "I need to be alone." She didn't glance back at him once as she walked to her back door.

Nate watched her go into her cottage and he heard the door slam shut once she was inside the house. With a deep sigh of regret, he maneuvered his vehicle toward his home. He hadn't helped her at all; he'd only caused her pain.

Once inside his house, he thought of the time he'd spent with her. It had been wonderful and he'd never felt happier. But now, clearly, she was angry with him. Would she ever forgive him for telling her about her past? Could he earn her love after he'd delivered the truth that had hurt rather than help her? It was ironic that by his being honest with her he'd ruined what they had shared. A close friendship that might have changed into something more. He already knew that he loved her more than he'd ever loved anyone, including Emily.

Was there anything he could do to make things right for her? Should he talk with someone about what he'd told her? Jonas? The preacher was the only one he'd consider confiding in. He'd known the man since he'd moved in with his grandparents as a young child. Nate knew Jonas much better now after having worked for him for the over three years.

Nate stood by his kitchen window, bent his head with eyes closed and prayed.

Please, Lord, help me to be the right man for her. Guide me into doing what is best for Abby even if I can't have the woman I love.

Chapter Eighteen

Seated at the end of her new bed in her cottage, Abby
cried. She felt betrayed by everyone in her life. By her
parents who weren't her parents. By Clara who wasn't her
schweschter. By Peter and the fact that no one she knew
had cared when she'd been hurt by Peter rejecting her for
Clara. She was even angry with *Endie* Rosemary and *Onkel*
Noah for having known the truth for years but never telling her. Yet, Noah had told Nate, a man who was basically
a stranger, someone he'd just met.

She sniffed, grabbed a tissue from her bed table and
blew her nose.

Abby couldn't help but be angry with Nate. He'd known
about her past before they'd left New Wilmington together
but he'd only decided to tell her this morning. And he'd
said it all in a beautiful park where she'd been enjoying the
greenery and the pond...until he'd told her some terrible
truths about her childhood...her family...her life.

She sobbed. The worse part was that she'd never get a
chance to talk to her real parents. They were gone, dead
and buried. She would never know what they'd looked like.
Or see their smile. Or feel the warmth of their love for her,
their only child.

"Why, Lord?" she cried out. Why had this happened

to them, to her? If her *mam* and *dat* were still alive, she wouldn't have felt misunderstood, unloved or blamed for the death of Dorothy's unborn child. Her heart ached for the loss of her baby cousin, but she had been just a baby when Dorothy—her aunt—had miscarried. How was that her fault?

Abby knew that she shouldn't be feeling sorry for herself. There had been good in her life, too. There were members of the Amish church community in New Wilmington who had been kind to her and supportive. Many of the parents of the children in school knew and appreciated that she helped the teacher in the classroom. And she'd valued her bond with Mae Mast and the woman's students she'd assisted in the classroom, everyone who'd given her purpose and the inspiration to become a full-time teacher.

She'd met and been loved by June and Jim Rhodes from the bakery where she worked…and then there were Michelle and George Palmer who had made her feel valued and cared for. They'd been indignant on her behalf when Dorothy's treatment of her had upset her too much for her to hide it.

Another thing to be grateful for was that she'd been hired as the new teacher for the New Berne school. And she was given a nice furnished place to live and a pony cart to use to get around town.

She thought of all the hard work Nate had done on the cottage. He'd done a fine job, and she was grateful for that, but Abby was still too upset with him to dwell on thoughts of him. She had the small thought that Nate hadn't deliberately hurt her but she forced it away.

Abby got up and went into the kitchen. Her stomach hurt and she realized that she had barely eaten that day. But even now, she couldn't eat, afraid that she'd feel sick with the pain of what she was feeling. Her throat was dry, so she filled a glass of water at the sink. The water was cool and quenched her thirst.

She sat in a chair in the living room and stared into space as she thought about Abram and Catherine Yost, the couple who'd given her life and loved her...and made sure she was safe in a homemade wooden baby seat strapped onto the back bench of their buggy. She'd never seen a child's seat like the one Nate had described, the one that had somehow saved her life when her parents had suffered and died.

Abby felt tears well in her eyes and she quickly blinked them away. Instead of crying, she would think about what they looked like and which part of her features she'd inherited from her father and mother.

She didn't know long she sat there. Abby realized that she must have fallen asleep, because from one blink to the next, the sky had gone from the sun low in the horizon filling the surrounding sky with orange to full darkness. With a gasp, she stood. After feeling her way into the kitchen, she found the edge of her countertop and the main section of cabinetry where she groped through drawers in her search for a flashlight. With a cry of delight, she found one. She clicked it on, enabling her to easily see her surroundings.

Exhaustion took hold of her. The journey from New Wilmington yesterday, her emotional encounter with her family and Peter, her recent anger with Nate, and the hours without eating had taken its toll. Abby unpinned her hair, fixed it into a long braid down her back and was soon in bed. As she lay on her pillow, she gazed up at the ceiling. Although she was tired, sleep didn't come easily to her.

I should call Noah and ask him for more information about my parents and the accident. Except she was afraid once she heard his voice, she'd become angry and say something she'd quickly regret.

What if she found a way to talk with Matthew, her uncle not her father she'd believed him to be. Would he tell her the truth? Describe her parents to her if she asked?

It wasn't a decision she could make now. She'd have to ponder on it tomorrow.

The next thing Abby became aware of was the daylight filtering into her cottage. The new day was here, and she'd managed to sleep despite her churning thoughts.

She got up and readied herself for the day. She put on a dress but didn't bother with a head covering. There was no need when she didn't plan on seeing anyone yet. She had decisions to make, phone calls to make…and grief to overcome.

Abby shook her head. Her *mam* and *dat* had been dead for twenty-two years. It was hard to believe that because she hadn't known they'd existed until now, she was mourning them for the first time.

Abby buttered two slices of bread she'd found in the pantry and made tea. The bread tasted like sawdust, even covered with salted butter. After she'd eaten her breakfast, she sipped her tea, taking the time to enjoy it properly, even though her thoughts spun with pain, anger and her struggle with feeling betrayed.

A heavy knock on her door startled. "Abby! It's me."

She knew his voice, which was unlike any other. "Go away, Nate. I need time alone."

"I'm worried about you," he said. It sounded like he was pressed against the door as if to get closer to her.

"Please leave and go about your day," she pleaded. "I'm fine."

He hesitated, then vowed, "I'll be back to check on you. This is my fault you're feeling this way."

Abby stilled. She hadn't expected him to take the blame for the pain she was feeling. Especially when it wasn't truly his fault. As hurt as she felt, she knew deep down that he hadn't done anything wrong. But she couldn't help but feel upset that he was the messenger, the one who'd told her everything. It was too embarrassing and shameful that he—or anyone—could see how much the truth was hurting her. She somehow felt broken in half.

"I'll be back," he promised and then he left.

A tiny spark of hope lit up her heart. He'd be back. She wasn't sure what that meant but she could only pray that whatever was in store for her in the future, it was better than the past.

Abby opened the window curtains and watched Nate head to the school then disappear inside. He was here and he was close. She also realized he'd been trying to help her by telling the truth—something her family hadn't been willing to do. And she loved him. How could she stay mad at him for being honest with her? The thought had her heart squeezing as her feelings for him washed over her. She loved him and she didn't want to lose him.

She needed the reminder that he was her friend, not her foe. Pulling back, she bent her head, closed her eyes and prayed for guidance and help in easing her pain.

She thought of her *mudder* and *vadder*, and she took comfort in knowing that they were in heaven watching over her, praying for her happiness from up above.

Nate studied all areas of the classroom and imagined the woman he loved teaching her students there. On the floor behind the desk were the two-by-sixes he planned to use for Abby's bookshelves. He'd been standing there for at least half an hour. He was having a difficult, emotional time this morning after Abby had sent him away.

I should have listened to Noah. But once Nate knew the truth, how could he keep it a secret from her? Abby deserved to know why she'd felt unloved and unappreciated growing up. Nate had hoped that he would be able to love her enough so that she'd be convinced she was valued and wanted. By him and everyone in his community. But mostly by him as the one who loved her the most.

What should he do? He couldn't stay away from her. They had grown too close. Maybe she needed a reminder of how much he cared about her.

He closed his eyes and prayed for guidance. Finally, he concluded that he couldn't stay here and work, not without making amends to her. He would apologize and explain why he'd told her what he'd learned. Remind her that she'd once told him that she trusted him enough to always be honest with her…that he'd never lie to her or keep things hidden. Like Peter had hidden his clandestine relationship with Clara.

All or nothing, he thought. He hoped for all but might end up with nothing. But he wouldn't give up, not when his future with her was at stake.

Nate abruptly left the school and strode back to her cottage. Rapping on the door, he waited and continued to seek help from *Gott* on how to handle this.

When she didn't answer, he knocked harder until finally Abby stood there in a pink dress, framed in the morning light with the sun shining on her blond hair. There were dark shadows under red eyes that told him she'd been crying for a while now. He took one long look into her beautiful green eyes and felt the sting of his own tears. He found to control his emotion but couldn't. This woman was too important to him.

"Abby," he whispered. "I'm sorry." He felt a tear escape to trail down his cheek. "I wouldn't hurt you for the world. I thought I was helping by telling you what your uncle told me." Nate stood there, agonizing that she would send him away again. "Please forgive me for hurting you. It's the last thing I wanted to do."

He saw her swallow hard. Abby stepped back and allowed him inside. He quickly closed the door behind him before he turned to gaze at her with the depth of his love. "Can we talk?" he asked hoarsely.

She gazed at him a long time before she finally nodded and gestured for him to sit.

"Spending time with you...going to the wedding...was enlightening and joyful," he began. "When I first offered to accompany you, it was because I felt your heartbreak and recognized it was something we shared. Then in the weeks before we went, I got a chance to know the real you... the sweet, caring woman who is kind and giving without expecting anything in return." He shook his head sadly. "You deserve more than what you've gotten in life, Abigail Yost. I may have offered you a chance to face your family at Clara's wedding with someone by your side, but it was I who benefited the most because I realized within days that you are everything I've ever wanted." He ran his fingers through his hair. Nate tried to figure out what she was thinking but then decided that it didn't matter. He would say his peace and hope for the best, trust in the Lord that everything would be all right.

He looked down at his hands in his lap as he drew a deep, calming breath before he released it. Nate captured her gaze and held it. "Abby, I don't want a fake relationship.

I haven't for weeks now, but I was afraid if I told you, then I'd lose you." Head bent low, she refused to meet his gaze, her fingers clenched on the tabletop. He shifted his chair closer, then dared to lay his hands over hers.

"I do want to end our fake relationship, Abby, but not because I want you out of my life. I want…and hope for something real with you. I want to marry you. I need you as my wife because…I'm deeply, endlessly in love with you." Tears filled his eyes again and spilled over. "Please, Abigail, forgive me for hurting you and let me spend the rest of my days making it up to you…and proving my love."

Abby hadn't said a word. Nate gazed into her eyes and there was no hint of her thoughts.

"Abby, please," he said, aching inside. "I love you."

She blinked and it was if brightness lit inside her, chasing away the stress and darkness. "Nate…" she whispered.

"I'm sorry." He was afraid. He never wanted to live another moment without her.

She shook her head. "I'm the one who is sorry. I blamed you for being who I wanted you to be. Honest and truthful. It's just that learning everything was a shock. And then I felt awful because I will never know my parents. I will never remember seeing them smile or having them hug me. Never hold on to memories of feeling my *mam*'s loving touch or witnessing my *dat*'s smile…or seeing them laugh and grin at each other at some shared amusement at something I did."

She turned her hands to entwine their fingers. "But none of that is your fault. If anything, you're the one who gave them back to me—a pair of loving parents I never even knew existed. You are an amazing man, Nate. You have watched out for me, done whatever you could to make me comfortable, and shown concern for me when I was upset.

You stepped up for someone who was barely more than a stranger when my sister came to scold me into attending her wedding…and you continued to be there for me every day after that." She inhaled sharply as her eyes filled with tears. "Nathaniel Hostetler, I love you. It didn't take me long to see your goodness, although at first I wasn't sure if we'd ever be friends. But look at us now. *Gott* has blessed us with each other."

"You will always have me if you want me," Nate said. "You are valued and loved, and you deserve a lifetime of happiness with a husband and a family." He grinned. "So, will you forgive me and be my betrothed? I want us to wed and have a forever future together."

Abby bit her lip as she gazed at him. "I… May I think about it?"

Nate felt a pit grow in his stomach. "*Ja*, I'll wait until you're ready, if you ever are."

She stood and walked the length of the kitchen and back again. "*Okey*, I'm ready now. *Ja*, I will be your betrothed… and I will be your wife for all times." She smiled. "As for forgiveness, there is nothing to forgive."

The pain in his belly went away and relief made him giddy. "I love you, Abby."

"I love you, Nate. Forever." She beamed at him and then giggled. "Until the Lord pulls us from this earth to enter through the gates of heaven."

He laughed, took her into his arms and kissed her. "Forever," he said and then he gently placed his lips over hers. He lifted his head and smiled as he pulled back. "You'll marry me soon, *oll recht*?"

She nodded. *"Ja."*

"I'll speak with Jonas tomorrow." He became concerned when she frowned. "What's wrong?"

"I don't have parents for him to ask permission," she said with sudden tears in her eyes. "I hope that doesn't stop us from marrying."

He briefly touched her cheek in comfort. "Not to worry, Abby. Your family already believe we were engaged. We'll figure it out. I'll always be there to figure things out with you. That's what a fiancé, a husband, is for."

Chapter Nineteen

"Abby and I would like to wed this November," Nate said with a calmness that surprised him. He'd gone straight to Preacher Miller's house after speaking to Abby and asked for a few minutes of his friend's time. He'd obliged, offering Nate a seat on the front porch.

"You would," Jonas said with a serious expression. Then he smiled at him warmly. "I'm sure we can get your marriage approved. November is the month for weddings, after all." The preacher regarded him with delight. "I'm happy for you, Nathaniel. I could see how much you and Abby care for each other."

Nate blushed. "*Ja*, I love Abby. She's a *wunderbor* woman. I'm eager to spend my life with her." He gazed at the man who was also his friend and employer. "I know you usually speak with a woman's parents to obtain permission from them first, but there is a problem that I'm hoping you can help us with."

The kind, older man frowned. "What kind of problem?"

"Asking for permission from Abby's parents isn't possible. Her *mam* and *dat* are deceased." Nate began to pace in the man's side yard. "She was raised by her aunt and uncle but they weren't...kind to her. She only learned recently that her *eldre* were killed in a tragic accident that Abby, as a baby, survived. Matthew Yost, the man she believed was her *vadder*, is her *vadder*'s younger *bruder*." Nate told Jonas everything he'd learned from her uncle Noah. "Getting betrothed is one thing but marrying is another. I don't know if they will allow us to wed."

The preacher looked thoughtful. "We must get permission from a family member. Do you think I should ask Matthew?"

"*Ja*, I believe he truly loves Abby, even if he rarely showed it over the years so he could keep the peace with his wife. I can reach out to the *English* couple who run the inn in New Wilmington where we stayed. Michelle and her husband, George, might be able to locate him and give us a way to contact him." Nate shook his head, unable to understand how anyone could not love Abby Yost. He explained why Dorothy had a problem with her niece.

"Thank the Lord that Abigail moved to our community," Jonas said as he placed his hand on Nate's shoulder. "Everyone thinks highly of her."

"I know I do. And she will always be loved by me," Nate promised.

The day after he'd called her, Nate heard back from Michelle Palmer with a number for a store where Matthew Yost used the phone. He would be calling Nate tomorrow at one. At twelve thirty on that day, he hurried to Jonas, and they both stood in the preacher's yard as they waited for the man's call.

Matthew called promptly at one. Nate handed Jonas his phone and he stepped away to give him the privacy needed in this situation. From several yards away, Nate waited, worried about what was being said. The preacher appeared serious with Nate's phone pressed to his ear. Finally, Jonas ended the call and approached Nate.

"Well?" Nate asked, his heart beating so hard it felt as if it was lodged in his throat.

"Matthew confessed a great deal while we talked." Jonas shook his head, amazing by whatever he'd learned. "The man is thrilled that you're in love with his niece. Said he could tell how much you love her. As for the two of you marrying…" He hesitated.

Nate swallowed hard. "*Ja?* And?"

Jonas grinned. "He gave permission for you two to marry. He knows you'll take *gut* care of her, giving her all the love she's never felt until you came along."

Nate felt his eyes fill with tears. "Matthew gave his permission?"

"*Ja*, he did." Jonas gazed at him intently. "Now I have one more person to talk with before your union happens."

Nate frowned. "Who?"

"Abigail Yost, of course." Jonas grinned. "Now go home. Stay away from the *schule* and the teacher's cottage. I'll be over to see you soon." He paused. "After I talk with the woman you love." He gave a nod toward his vehicle. "Go now."

"*Oll recht.*" Nate left. He was, as always, eager to see Abby again, but he would be obedient because he trusted Jonas. It helped him to know that Jonas had both his and Abby's best interests at heart.

It had been a day since Nate had spoken with the preacher. After his conversation with Jonas, Nate had returned to the cottage to let her know that Jonas said that it was necessary to get permission from a family member. The man she loved then told her that he'd called the Palmers for help in finding a way to contact Matthew. What if the man she'd always believed was her father refused to give his blessing for her and Nate to marry?

When Preacher Jonas appeared at her cottage door, Abby immediately worried that something had gone wrong.

"Abigail," he greeted. "May I come in?"

"Of course," she said with a smile. She stepped back and invited him to sit. "I take it you spoke with Nate?"

Jonas nodded. "I did. Yesterday. We reached out to Matthew in New Wilmington to ask his permission for Nate and you to wed."

Abby frowned. "You did? And did you get it?"

"I did," he said. "Matthew is happy for you and Nate. He believes Nate is a *gut* man who is in love with you and who will make you a fine husband, loving and protecting you for all the days of your lives. He believes that your happiness is long overdue and he is sorry."

"He said all that?" Abby waited with hope in her heart.

"He did," Jonas said.

At his answer, she could barely contain her happiness. "*Danki.* I feel so blessed."

The preacher inclined his head. "You are blessed, but then so are we for having you in our community." He stood. "I should get back. I need to see Nate again, and the two of you have a wedding to plan."

Abby's joy dimmed. "I don't have anyone to give us a reception," she said sadly.

"Of course, you do," Jonas insisted. "You have us…your new community. The only things you and Nate need to do is decide is who your attendants will be and which people from New Wilmington you wish to invite."

She beamed at him. "*Danki* again, Jonas," she said as

she followed him outside. "And you're not to worry—I still plan to teach *schule* for at least a year or two."

"Praise the Lord," he replied before he left.

Abby couldn't wait to talk with Nate. She wanted—needed—to see him. Before she had a chance to call him, he arrived with a grin on his face to share in their joy for their upcoming union.

School started during the first week of September. Thanks to Nate, her classroom was ready, and there were textbooks and all the necessary supplies on the bookshelves he'd built for her. Abby greeted her students with a smile on her face.

She had a list of their names and what grades they were in. Abby broke them into four groups separating them by age, from the youngest children at five years old to the oldest students who were in eighth grade and due to leave school at the end of this teaching year. The students were eager to learn and happy to be in a classroom closer to their homes. After a morning of lessons for each group, Abby dismissed them for lunch.

She opened the door for them to go outside. Nate had re-done the picnic table in the back and built another two for the schoolyard. There was a new swing set in a fenced-in area, which she knew the children would gravitate to once they finished their lunch. To her surprise, Nate appeared at her door as the last child filed outside.

"Nate!" she cried, happy to see him. "I was just going to eat lunch."

He held up a brown paper bag. "I brought mine as well. I thought we could enjoy this time together."

They walked to the back and sat side by side at one end of the new picnic table. Some of the children had already eaten and were running to the swing set while others started a game of baseball in a grassy area away from the swings. Abby beamed at her fiancé, thankful once again for having him in her life.

"I gave a list of the guests we'd like to invite to our wedding to Fannie," Nate said.

She arched her eyebrow. "You did? I wasn't sure we were done going over everyone."

"Abby," he said, as he reached to cover her hand with his own. "It will be fine. I know the people you feel are important enough to invite. The list includes the Rhodeses, the Palmers, Noah and Rosemary Yost with their daughter Ruth Ann. We talked about Dorothy and Matthew and decided to invite them despite your past with them. If Dorothy doesn't want to attend, that's fine. I believe that Matthew will want to be there and will come even if Dorothy stays at home. And you wanted to invite Clara and Peter, especially after they both apologized to you."

Abby nodded. "It's really happening," she whispered with joy and love filling her heart because of Nate Hostetler, an amazing man. "You and I are going to be man and wife."

"We are." His smile was wide. "It's you and me forever."

She nodded. "I love you, Nathaniel Hostetler," Abby said with a smile.

He beamed at her with love and affection in his bright, light brown eyes. "And I love you, Abigail Yost soon-to-be Abby Hostetler, my bride."

The months before the wedding seemed to fly by. On the morning of the day that she and Nate would exchange vows, Abby felt nervous. She was eager to marry the man she loved—it was having to deal with family on both sides that concerned her. Everyone from New Wilmington they'd invited had come, including Matthew, Dorothy, and Clara with Peter. But the people she most wanted to see and share this special time with were the friends who'd supported her when she'd needed to feel better about herself throughout the years. Michelle and George Palmer. June and Jim Rhodes. And from her family...there were Noah, Rosemary and their daughter, Abby's cousin—Ruth Ann. And she was looking forward to seeing Mae Mast again and her husband Josiah.

Abby had asked Ruth Ann to be her attendant. Nate's best man was his older brother Aaron, who returned for the occasion with a woman he'd recently married in Indiana. As they drove up to Jonas and Alta Miller's place where the ceremony was to take place, Abby studied her betrothed and thought he was handsome in his Sunday best dress of white shirt, black vest and pants with black shoes. On his head, he wore his wide-brimmed black felt hat. She ran her gaze along his clean-shaven jawline and envisioned how he would look once they were wed, with the beard all Amish men grew once they married. Seated close beside her, she detected his clean, masculine scent...of soap, shampoo and something that belonged uniquely to him, which she loved.

Nate turned his head and their eyes connected. "You look beautiful, Abby. I love that color of light blue on you. It brings out other colors in your green eyes and highlights your blond hair. But then I love everything you wear, because there isn't anything that would take away from your beauty."

She chuckled. "I was thinking something similar about you, except you're more handsome than any man I've ever met...and your appeal is inside as well as outside."

Abby heard a snort from Nate's older brother Aaron, and

she turned to him with an eyebrow raised. "You've never felt that way about Beth?"

Aaron became silent for a moment. "I have."

"Well, then, hush," she said teasingly. "I'm allowed to say what I need to say to the man I'm about to marry... for love."

After the wedding ceremony, they would head to the Bontrager property, where Micah and his wife, Katie, were hosting the reception in their barn, a space large enough to hold all the wedding guests. The feast, she was told, had been prepared by a joint effort by the members of their community who had graciously welcomed her into their midst.

She was slightly nervous, but not because of Nate. Abby was grateful for his comforting presence beside her on the rear bench seat of his brother's family buggy. She couldn't wait to be his wife.

Aaron drove them and her cousin Ruth to the Millers and parked close to the house. Nate and Abby climbed out first and headed into the backyard where chairs were set up in rows with a wooden pulpit facing the front of con-gregation. Abby drew a calming breath as she walked with Nate to the chairs reserved for the groom and bride-to-be.

"Are you ready to be my wife, *liebchen*?" Nate whis-pered in her ear.

She nodded. "*Ja.* Ready and eager," she murmured with a smile, pleased that he'd called her "my love."

The ceremony went off without a hitch. As she and Nate left their seats, Abby noticed her Uncle Matthew sitting next to his brother Noah. She met Matthew's gaze and saw him smile. He appeared genuinely happy for her. Abby gave him a nod before she walked with Nate back to Aaron's buggy, which would transport the newlyweds and their attendants to the reception.

Katie and Fannie were there with their babies, who already looked too big for a month old. The friends had given birth within days of each other in October.

Abby and Nate were seated next to each other in the *Eck* with their attendants by their sides. She watched the guests file into the room, happily noting the Rhodeses and Palmers who sat close to each other. Noah, Rosemary and Matthew sat along one side of the U-shaped table formation, but near the end with Dorothy, Clara and Peter. Beth was seated next to Aaron on his other side.

The food that was brought out was delicious—the usual wedding meal of chicken, celery and stuffing casserole. There were large platters of different vegetables that made their way to everyone in the room, starting with the bride and groom. Abby smiled as her gaze ran over their guests and noticed someone she didn't recognize.

"Who's that?" she whispered to Noah, leaning close.

"Who?" Nate breathed.

"That man over there. He seems familiar but I can't place him." She gestured to a tall man with brown hair and eyes who sat on the end of the *Eck* on Nate's side.

Abby heard him gasp when he finally caught sight of the man in question. "Praise the Lord. I never thought we'd see him again," he said, emotion thick in his voice.

"Nate?" she eyed him with concern before she turned to stare at the man again. She realized why he looked familiar—it was because he resembled Aaron and Nate. "He's related to you, isn't he?"

Her husband nodded. *"Ja."*

Nate had told her about his oldest married brother. Nate hadn't seen Sam in nearly thirteen years.

"Your eldest *bruder*!" she exclaimed softly, for his ears alone, mindful of others within distance watching them. Then, aware of her new husband's stunned disbelief, she got up from the table and approached the man. "Welcome home, Sam Hostetler. Your *bruder* and I are glad you're here."

The wonders of *Gott* never ceased to amaze, Abby thought. Today was her wedding to Nate, the happiest day in her life. And now to top off their joy, Nate's brother Samuel had returned to New Berne.

Thanks be to *Gott*.

Abby returned to Nate and gave him a special smile. "I love you, *mein mon*."

"I love you, *mein frau*," Nate returned with a loving expression. "Forever."

"And ever," she replied with a grin. "We have a lot to look forward to."

She gazed at the man she loved…and she could see her future clearly now.

Epilogue

Three years later

Abby was busy all morning cleaning when she heard Nate call her. "Abby!"

She smiled as she smoothed the bedcovers into place before she moved through the house on their farm—the one Nate had purchased just over three years ago. "I'm coming!"

Living here was exactly as Abby had hoped—wonderfully warm and homey. Her beloved husband stood at the open back door, staring at the pasture where their Holstein dairy cows grazed the rich, lush green mixture of grass, clover and alfalfa.

She stepped outside. "What do you need?"

He turned to her with an affectionate smile as he gazed lovingly from her head down to her baby bump. "There is something I want to show you in the barn if you're up to it."

Abby laughed. "Of course, I am. Our little one isn't due for two weeks." Since she'd become pregnant, Nate had been overly concerned with her welfare and refused to allow her to help with any farm chores. She studied her handsome husband, loving everything about him. She'd never expected to be this happy, but her husband showed her every day how much he loved and cared for her.

"You're my world, Abigail Hostetler. You know that, *recht*?"

"I know and feel the same way about you," she said with a heart full of love for this kind, genuine man of honor. "So, what is it you want to show me?"

"Abby—"

"You called me out here," she reminded him. "And now you're making me wait when it's obvious you're excited about something." She studied his beloved features with his warm light brown eyes filled with affection for her.

Nate gently caught her hand and tugged her toward the milking barn and the area fenced off for pregnant cows.

The scent of the animals was stronger inside the outbuilding. He tugged her gently toward the back of the milking area toward the place where the cows who would soon give birth rested. He stopped suddenly and gently turned her shoulders to face an animal there. "Look!" he urged.

"*Ach!* She had her calf!" Abby exclaimed, loving how the little one struggled to its feet but stood close to his mother on wobbly, spindly legs. "How adorable!"

Nate chuckled. "Only you would think a bull calf is adorable."

"And you don't?" she challenged as she faced him. She knew the truth about this man, her husband, who allowed only her to see him cry when he became overwhelmed by emotion.

He sighed. "*Ja*, I think he's cute."

"Sam," she decided. "His name is Sam."

"Come on," Nate said with amusement as with a light tug he led her to an area at the far back corner of the barn. "Sam's mother isn't the only one who gave birth today." He pointed to another cow and her calf. "See? This one's a heifer calf."

Abby gasped. This calf had yet to stand up. She lay on

folded legs near the mother, who was licking her little one clean.

"Joanna," she whispered with reverence as she focused on the newborn.

When she glanced back at her husband, he was shaking his head. "You managed to come up with names for the new calves," he commented, "but none for our unborn child."

"There's plenty of time for that," Abby asserted.

"Only two weeks," he reminded her. "We need to do it now."

"Fine," she said with a grin. "For a boy, I like Benjamin. And for a girl, I think Faith would be a sweet name for our *dochter*." Abby searched her husband's expression but he gazed at her without showing his thoughts. "You don't like them," she said with sudden tears in her eyes. Why did she feel so much more emotional since she'd gotten pregnant?

"Abby." Nate's tone was gentle as if he could tell she was struggling. "Abby, I love the names you've chosen. *Liebchen*, I mean it. They are perfect for our *soohn* or *dochter*."

He took her hand and entwined his fingers with hers. "Let's go back to the *haus*."

As he escorted her back, she felt a squeezing pain along her abdomen through to her back, sharp enough to make her gasp and stop.

"Abby?" Nate eyed with her concern and she saw the fear in his brown eyes.

"I'm fine, but I think our baby is ready to be born," she assured him calmly. Holding her stomach, she took big, even breaths.

Nate nodded. "I'll call the midwife."

Nate paced his living room while he waited for Abby to give birth.

"Nate?" His eldest brother entered the house and saw him.

"What are doing here?" Nate asked.

"Returning this." His brother smiled as he held up Nate's utility stapler. "Where's your wife?"

Nate grinned. "She's having a baby. The midwife is with her."

"Did you two finally pick out names?" Sam sat on the sofa.

"*Ja*, after she named two of our new calves. The heifer calf is Joanna." Nate had to bite his tongue to keep from laughing. "And the bull calf is Sam."

"Sam, huh?" Sam then burst out in loud guffaws and Nate joined him.

He nodded. *"Ja."*

"Must be one magnificent calf," Sam said.

"Nate?" The midwife stood in the the hallway.

Nate's eyes flashed to her, full of hope. *"Ja?"*

The woman smiled. "Your wife has given birth to a beautiful healthy daughter weighing seven pounds, five ounces, and she's eighteen inches long."

"I'm a father?" Nate blinked rapidly as he was hit with a rush of relief and joy. "A baby girl! And my wife…?"

"You'd be proud of Abby. She's fine. Her labor came fast and hard, but she held strong, determined to quickly bring your *dochter* into the world to meet you." With a grin, she waved her hand. "Follow me."

He glanced back at Sam, who smiled and looked happy for him as he nodded for him to go to his wife.

The first thing he saw was his beautiful wife in bed, propped up on pillows, their baby resting in the curve of her arm. She appeared sleepy but satisfied. As soon as she caught sight of him, Abby flashed him a huge smile.

"Come and meet Faith, your *dochter*," she invited warmly.

Nate couldn't keep his eyes off them as he slowly approached the bed. "Abby…"

His wife held his gaze. "You won't hurt her. Come closer."

He reached her bedside and bent his head to give Abby a kiss. Then he settled the gentlest of kisses on their newborn daughter's forehead. "Our baby girl is so beautiful." It felt as if a burst of sunshine had warmed him inside and out. "Abby, I love you and I love little Faith."

He tugged a chair closer to the bed to sit, needing to be closer to her. He would stay by his wife's side even after she fell asleep. "So beautiful," he murmured.

"*Ja*, she is," Abby murmured.

"I was talking about you, although the same does apply to our baby." After ensuring that his wife was fine, Nate studied Faith. Their baby slept with her eyes closed. "I wonder what color her eyes are."

"We won't know for some time," Abby said. "I've been told that eye color frequently changes as a baby grows older." She smiled. "It usually happens between six and eight months."

Nate nodded. "Something about the eyes getting light after being in the dark for nine months, *recht*?"

"*Ja.*" She eyed him with love and affection, and once again he felt as if he was the happiest man alive. "She has your brown hair."

He nodded. "But that can change, too."

"True. I hope it doesn't," Abby said, "I love the color of your hair." With her free hand, she reached out to touch him.

"She is beautiful, *Mam*." Nate noticed how tired his wife was and wondered if his presence was keeping her up when she should be sleeping. "Do you want me to take her?" He was nervous about the prospect. He was afraid he'd do something that would hurt his newborn child. Then his gaze fell on the hospital bassinet on the other side of his wife's bed.

"You want to hold her?" she asked.

He firmed his resolve. "You need a break. I need to learn how to help you with our Faith."

"She's sleeping," Abby said as she held on to his gaze. "You can put her in her bassinet if you'd rather. Just a few more minutes and then she is all yours."

"She already is," he whispered with tears in his eyes. "You both are."

* * * * *

*If you enjoyed this story
by Rebecca Kertz,
Read Esther's story in*
A Convenient Christmas Wife
*Available now from Love Inspired!
Discover more at LoveInspired.com*

Dear Reader,

Abigail Yost is the newly hired schoolteacher in the Amish community of New Berne, Pennsylvania. Heartbroken by her ex-betrothed's betrayal, Abby is pleased for a chance to start a new life away from her home community. But then her sister, Clara, the woman who stole her fiancé, demands that Abby attend their wedding, even though she doesn't want to go. No one in her family cares that she's been hurt. After being pressured, Abby is forced to agree.

Nathaniel Hostetler is working at the school and the cottage, preparing both for the new schoolteacher and the first day of classes. At first, he and Abby are at odds with each other, but then Nate learns the truth about her background and realizes that she suffered heartbreak as he did when the girl he loved chose another. After hearing Abby's conversation with her sister who showed up out of the blue, he offers to help her by pretending to be her fiancé at the wedding so everyone will realize that she has moved on from her ex. But now Nate and Abby need to convince their New Berne community before they leave for the wedding.

It was a joy for me to write Nate and Abby's story. I hope you enjoyed their book.

I wish you good health and happiness!

Blessings and light,
Rebecca Kertz